Spy!

Also by Anna Myers

Anna Myers

Walker & Company
New York

First published in the United States of America in 2008 by
Walker Publishing Company, Inc.
Visit Walker & Company's Web site at www.walkeryoungreaders.com

For information about permission to reproduce selections from this book, write to
Permissions, Walker & Company, 175 Fifth Avenue, New York, New York 10010

Library of Congress Cataloging-in-Publication Data
Myers, Anna.
Spy! / Anna Myers. — 1st ed.
p.   cm.
Summary: In 1774, twelve-year-old Jonah becomes a pupil of Nathan Hale, who
inspires him to question his beliefs about the impending revolution, and two years
later, Jonah makes a decision that leads to Nathan's execution.
ISBN-13: 978-0-8027-9742-1 • ISBN-10: 0-8027-9742-3
1. Hale, Nathan, 1755–1776—Juvenile fiction. [1. Hale, Nathan, 1755–1776—Fiction.
2. Teachers—Fiction. 3. Spies—Fiction. 4. Orphans—Fiction. 5. Connecticut—
History—Revolution, 1775–1783—Fiction. 6. United States—History—Revolution,
1775–1783—Fiction.] I. Title.
PZ7.M9814Spy 2008   [Fic]—dc22   2008000254

Book design by Daniel Roode
Typeset by Westchester Book Composition
Printed in the U.S.A. by Quebecor World Fairfield
2 4 6 8 10 9 7 5 3 1

For Elizabeth Joy Myers

You are a special treasure who came to us in May. How blessed we are to have a dimpled, blue-eyed baby girl come to be part of our family. At seven months you look mostly like your mother and her mother, and that will make you a beautiful lady. There is a special sweetness in your smile that I believe will always be there. How fortunate I feel to live only two blocks from you now so that I can see that smile often. You will grow up sweet, but you will grow up strong too. Welcome to our world, little treasure. It will be a better world because of you!

> Love,
> Nana

WELCOME: to my daughter

You came into a year of rain,
wet thing,
tiny
as a frog
in the palm,

laughing with the odd
angles of this world:
elbows, Pisa
crooks in the cottonwood tree—
all tucked in
the off-center grin
you take from my father

and opening like sudden
sunshine on one
side of a pitched tin roof,
spilling down on the dandelions
below.

—Ben Myers

The End

This is a story that begins at the end.
It is a story of a man who was too young
and of a boy who grew suddenly old.

CHAPTER ONE

The Boy

The hanging would take place at eleven. The boy, Jonah, wished it could happen at night, or at least in the evening, when he might have stayed unnoticed in the shadows, but he was forced to hunker low behind the rock wall. If the soldiers saw him, what would they do? Would they hurl stones, or maybe flog him with the awful whip called a cat-o'-nine-tails? The boy bit at his lower lip and pressed himself close against the ground. If they thrashed him, his wounds would stop bleeding and eventually heal. If they hit him with stones, he could take the pain. What he could not endure, though, was being driven away. He must be present for the death of this man he loved, must bear witness until the end.

The drumbeat came to him, and he knew they were coming. The boy's heart sounded loud in his ears, almost as loud as the drum. He eased his body up so that he could see above the wall, but no one was in sight yet. The apple tree stood undisturbed, some of the red fruit still hanging from its branches.

Jonah had heard the news in the tavern. "Reckon they'll use the apple tree to hang him." The soldier had shaken his head as he spoke. "Seems a shame, him so young and all." He shrugged. "Still, a spy gets caught and he hangs; everyone knows that!"

For a moment the boy froze. The soldier was wrong. Not everyone knew that spies were hanged. He had not known. Jonah made himself move. He had just carried a dish to the soldiers' table, and his hand trembled as he set the plate down. "Who?" he asked. "Who will they hang?"

The soldier looked up at him. "Wasn't talking to you, now, was I?"

Jonah had been holding his breath, but he let it go and murmured, "No, sir."

"Ain't no secret, now is it, Denton?" the other soldier said. He looked up at Jonah. The soldier had a great red blotch on one side of his face. It was a fact Jonah noticed, but one that he did not think about until much later. "It's Captain Nathan Hale, boy. Caught him last night trying to sneak through the lines. Almost got away with it too, he did, but they say he was betrayed by someone close to him."

Jonah felt the shaking that had been in his hands spread throughout his body, but he tried to hold himself still. "When?" he asked. "When will they hang Captain Hale? Please, sir, can you tell me?"

The first soldier had his mouth full of eggs, but he

spoke anyway. "Bloody interested in a rebel hanging, ain't you, boy? You know this Hale?"

"Yes, sir." Jonah's voice was soft. "He was my teacher back in Connecticut, before the war."

"A schoolmaster?" the second soldier asked. "He seems no more than a boy his own self. I've seen him, I have. How old is he, do you reckon?"

"Twenty, I think, or twenty-one." Jonah did not look at the soldiers as he spoke.

The first soldier laughed and slapped his hand on the table. "Shame weren't nobody to teach him! Guess he knows now what happens to them that try to spy on the king's regulars."

Jonah had to ask again. "But when will they hang him?"

"Eleven this morning, that's the word, over in Artillery Park." The second soldier, the one with the red blotch, looked kindly at the boy and went back to his breakfast.

The first soldier scowled up at Jonah. "We'll be on duty, we will. Don't want to see the likes of you hanging about. You've no business to be there, you being a loyal subject to King George. You be that, right, boy? No matter who was your teacher?"

"Yes, sir," said Jonah, and trying not to run, he retreated.

In the kitchen, he stood, breathing hard. For a moment, he leaned against the big table with its pile of dishes and pans. Then he untied the apron strings fastened behind his back and lifted it from around his neck. The tavern owner would find the apron in a wad on top of the dirty dishes. He would also find his customers complaining that no serving boy had tended to their needs. Jonah would lose his job, and Mr. Samuel would be notified. No matter! He flung himself through the open back door. He did not know what time it was. He did not know where Artillery Park might be in this strange city. One thing he did know. He must be in that spot before eleven.

And he was, crouched behind the low wall and listening now to the drumbeats that foretold the coming soldiers. When the sound grew stronger, Jonah eased up for another look. There he was, Master Hale, his hands bound behind his back, and hanging around his neck a coiled rope. Jonah saw the noose that dangled from the end of the rope, and for a moment the world went dark before his eyes. He swayed against the wall, afraid he might faint. "Don't," he whispered to himself. "You have to see."

A boy, maybe slightly older than Jonah, walked in front, beating a drum. Two soldiers walked on either side of Master Hale, and one, with a red-blotched face, walked behind. Each clutched a bayonet, pointed at their prisoner. Next came a cart driven by the soldier who had threatened Jonah.

He clenched his fists. If only he had a gun. Could he have gotten somehow into the soldiers' camp and stolen one? Probably not. Besides, he could not stop the hanging. He would have been killed himself, of course, and still the hanging would have gone right on, probably not more than minutes behind schedule. There was nothing he could do for Master Hale, nothing but bear witness. He drew in a long breath. He would not faint. Jonah had not, at first, been able to look at his teacher's face. Now he did.

Nathan Hale showed no sign of anguish. His blue eyes looked straight ahead as he moved. The September sun touched his fair hair and seemed almost to form a halo about his head. A small crowd of people had gathered in front of the apple tree, and the boy decided to join them. The soldiers from the tavern would be too busy with the terrible task to notice him.

Jonah stood, put his hands on the wall, and vaulted over. He landed near a large woman who turned briefly to stare at him. "Watch yourself there, you little bugger."

The smaller woman beside her made a sort of snorting sound. "Young ones running wild all over the place," she said. Then she leaned forward. "My eyes ain't that strong these days, you know, but he don't look so much like a spy to me, not a'tall like a dark sneak, I'd say."

The big woman shook her head. "He's guilty, though. They say he confessed. Still, it's a pity, him so young. Not a mother in this city, loyalist or no, wouldn't have her heart touched to see him. Let us not tarry." The women turned and moved away.

Jonah found himself almost at the front now. Only a couple of men blocked his vision. Squeezing around them, he stood boldly in the first line. The soldiers halted beside the apple tree, and the man on the cart stopped his horse exactly beneath the largest branch. The driver hopped down from the cart. First he folded down a set of steps. Next, he took the rope from Master Hale's shoulders and carried it back up the steps. He threw the end over the limb and tied two knots. The rope dropped now from the tree, and Jonah watched the deadly swing of the noose.

A British officer, who had ridden up on a horse, dismounted. "Up with you," he ordered, and the soldiers poked at Master Hale with their bayonets.

Jonah felt his stomach roll, and he put his hand over his mouth in case his breakfast came up. The drum began to beat slowly. It was hard for the prisoner to mount even the short steps with his hands bound behind him, and Jonah feared with each climb that Master Hale would slip.

When Master Hale stood on top of the cart bed, the driver took the noose and the prisoner bent so that the shorter man could slip the rope over his head and tighten it about his neck.

On the ground, the officer took a step forward, unrolled a piece of paper, and read, "Hear ye, hear ye, by the order of General William Howe, army of King George, one Nathan Hale, a captain in the rebel army, having confessed to being a spy, is to be hanged by the neck until dead. This 22nd day of September in the year of our Lord, 1776." The driver was back on the seat and ready to drive the cart from beneath Master Hale's feet.

The officer stepped back, turned his head up toward the prisoner. "Any last words from you, rebel?"

The young man looked down from the cart at the people in front of him. Jonah felt his teacher's eyes meet his own, and for a fraction of a second a smile played on the prisoner's lips. Then he glanced toward heaven and spoke. "I only regret that I have but one life to lose for my country." Murmurs rose up from the crowd, and Jonah saw tears on the cheeks of the British soldier who stood near Master Hale. Before the soldier had a chance to lift the reins to drive the cart from beneath him, the young prisoner stepped up and off the cart. His body jerked and swayed at the end of the rope.

Jonah felt his own body jerk violently. He dropped his gaze to stare at the ground, and he dug at the earth with the toe of his boot. Don't look at him, he told himself, but still out of the corner of his eye he was aware of the terrible swaying of the form. Despite the bright sun, Jonah felt an awful cold come upon him, and his teeth started to chatter. He wrapped his arms around his body. How long does it take to kill a person by hanging? He hoped Master Hale was unconscious. Perhaps he could tell by looking at his face, but he could not make himself do that.

Finally, after what seemed a very long time, the officer spoke. "It is over," he announced. He swung up onto his horse and rode away.

No one in the small crowd moved. "Disperse now; go on with you," called one of the soldiers, and a few people started to step away.

Jonah did not want to move, and besides, his feet felt too heavy to lift. He did not look up at his former teacher, but the shadow of his swinging body fell on the boy. "Cut him down," he shouted. "Cut him down now!"

The soldiers all turned to stare at him. "What's this?"

called one soldier. "Does a boy now shout out orders to the king's men?"

"Cut him down," Jonah said again. "He's dead now. Why don't you cut him down?"

"He stays there, you little fool," said a soldier. "The spy will hang for days, a warning to others."

"I know you!" called the soldier from the cart. He jumped down from the seat and advanced toward Jonah. "You're the little scoundrel from the tavern. Didn't I charge you not to show your face here? You'll learn to listen to what you're told, you will, and it will be me as sees to that lesson." The soldier waved his arms at the boy.

Still, Jonah did not move, not until a heavy slap across his face made his head jolt. He turned then and ran. Pushing around a man who stood in his way, he fled down the street, then down a different one. Through street after street he ran, never looking where his feet fell or at the buildings on either side of him.

The night before, he had been aware of the fire that raged in the lower part of the city, but from his spot in the inn, Jonah had been untouched by it. Now he ran down roads where fires still smoldered, ran past blackened walls that had once been homes or shops. People poked about in the ruins, but nothing made him linger longer than was necessary to catch a smoke-filled breath. He had no idea where to go, yet he did not stop moving, not until he smelled the sea. He slowed when the salty breeze came to him, slowed and looked. The sea was familiar. He had known the smell of the sea all his life, had sat beside the sea back in Connecticut, back in New London.

His nose led him down the right path, and he threw himself down on a large rock. Gulls cried over his head, and not far away two men fished from a small boat. Jonah liked the rock, liked the sights and sounds, and most of all the smell of the water.

How long had he run through the streets of New York? He studied the sun and knew the time was well into afternoon. Mister Samuel must have been notified by now, and Mercy too. Jonah hated to worry his sister, but he knew he would not go back to the inn. He would sit beside the water at least until the sun disappeared. Maybe he would even spend the cool night shivering on the rock beside the sea. He could not go back to the inn, not tonight, not ever.

CHAPTER TWO

The Man

New London, Connecticut, March 1774

Nathan Hale bent over the hearth and blew on the fire he had just started. He wanted the flames to burn high so that the small building would be warm when his scholars came. This was not his first job. That had been at East Haddam, where he had held classes for a term. Still, he was young, only nineteen, and his heart was full of a young man's dreams. He would mold the boys who would soon enter this little red schoolhouse. He would teach them Latin and literature. He would open their eyes to the world around them, a world much larger than this town of New London, much larger than the colony of Connecticut. He would give them a love of learning, and their lives would never be the same.

His father had hoped he would become a minister. In fact, that was why Deacon Hale had educated two of his sons, sending them off together to Yale College. Enoch, two years older, had followed that path to the ministry, his Bible in his hand, but Nathan had chosen instead to teach. He loved teaching, yet there remained in him a restlessness, a searching for something more.

The fire blazed high now. The schoolmaster stood and moved toward the front of the room. Pausing for a moment near the window, he scanned the bare trees on the schoolhouse hillside and the frozen stream below; no sign of spring. He moved on to the tall desk. Three books lay about in various spots where he had left them. Picking up the volumes, he ran his hand slowly over each one before stacking it in the corner. He would open these books and open the minds of his boys and maybe some girls too. He smiled. "Let me advise you a bit, Cousin," Samuel had told him two days ago when he had first come to New London. "Keep your strange ideas about educating females to yourself. People here won't take to such nonsense."

Nathan had resisted asking how New London took to Tories. It bothered him, this cousin of his being so doggedly loyal to King George. "You'll get to know your cousin Samuel," Deacon Hale had said when Nathan agreed to keep school in New London.

Samuel, who had always lived in Massachusetts, had come only a few years earlier to the Connecticut town to take over the whalebone mill that had once belonged to his wife's father. Nathan could remember meeting his older cousin only once many years before, but he remembered that Samuel had been kind to him then.

He saw that same kindness in Samuel's eyes still. His cousin was kind, kind but blind, Nathan thought. Samuel was too blind to see that the English Parliament had no right to place taxes on the people of the colonies, people who were not represented in that Parliament. Samuel was too blind to see that it was time to force Parliament and king to stop treading on the rights of the colonists.

The sound of an opening door made Nathan forget his cousin. He moved to greet his first scholar. "Have I come too early? I wanted to get here before the others." A small dark-haired boy stepped into the building and took off his hat.

"You're never too early for learning." He reached out to take the boy's cold hand. "I am Master Hale," he said. "What is your name, my good fellow?"

"Jonah," said the boy, and he shook his teacher's hand. "My name is Jonah Hawkins, but I'm not properly here."

"You're not properly here?" Nathan smiled at the boy. "I am afraid you will need to explain that statement to your schoolmaster."

The boy looked down. "I'm not paid for, that's the whole of it, so I can't stay. My father has been ailing, and . . ." He paused for a moment. "No payment was sent to the proprietors for this term. My father doesn't rightly know I've come." The boy's lip trembled, and Nathan knew he fought tears. "You see, sir, I wanted to meet you, so I could . . ." He paused again. "You might say, imagine things at school, the others learning and all, I mean."

"Come in, Master Jonah Hawkins." Nathan waved his

arm in a welcoming gesture. He'd talk to the men who managed Union School. This boy would be among his students. He'd see to it even if he had to pay the proprietors' bill from his own meager wages. "Come in," he said again, but the boy did not move another step.

"I said I can't pay, sir."

"We'll work something out, Jonah. Let me worry about that."

The boy shook his head. "My father would never agree to charity."

"Can you not spend just today with us?" He would think of something later. There had to be a way.

"One day wouldn't be charity, not so much, would it, sir?"

"Decidedly not, but are you expected at home? Will your absence cause someone to fret?"

The boy shook his head. "My father has gone with my sister for a stay at my aunt's house in the country. I'm at home for the cow and the chores." His face grew sad. "My mother is dead these two years now."

"I lost my own mother when I was young, Jonah. My father later married again, and the lady became a kind mother to us all."

"My father won't marry again," said the boy.

"Why such certainty?"

The boy's voice was low. "My father is dying, sir. It's something I know, although I still pray it won't be so."

"I will beseech God with that same petition, Jonah." Nathan put his arm around the boy's thin shoulders. "Now, for today you shall have use of my own hornbook."

"I shan't need a hornbook, sir." Jonah held his head high. "I am among the Latin scholars."

Nathan was surprised. The boy must be older than he looked. "A Latin scholar, are you? How old are you, Jonah?"

"Twelve, sir. I know I'm small, but I am strong." His cheeks turned red. "Forgive me for boasting."

"It's all right, Jonah."

"Master Tracy would have rapped my knuckles for the sin of pride," said the boy, and he looked down at his hands, remembering, Nathan supposed, many such punishments.

"Master Tracy is not here, and you won't find me one for rapping knuckles."

The boy smiled. "That will make a change, sir."

"Oh, don't misunderstand, Jonah." The teacher folded his arms across his chest and raised one eyebrow. "I expect my scholars to behave themselves as gentlemen, but I have no plans to resort to physical punishments. I kept the East Haddam school last term and found no boy there in need of having his knuckles rapped. I would assume New London boys are as well behaved."

"Oh yes, sir."

The sound of boys' laughter and shouts came to their ears. "Other pupils are arriving." Nathan moved to the window. There they were, streams of boys climbing the hill. Most of them carried a stick of firewood. Smaller boys had hornbooks tied about their neck or stuck under their arms. He drew in a long breath. He was ready, ready for all thirty of them.

Spy!

He opened the door, and immediately the crowd grew quiet. "One at a time, gentlemen," he said. "I am Master Hale. Each of you will step up, tell me your name, hang you coats and hats in the cloakroom, and find your place at one of the tables; older scholars at the back please."

The last boy, seven-year-old Timothy Green, trembled when he put his hand in Nathan's. "I've never been to school before," he said, "and I don't know very much. My mother said I should learn from her first, but my father wanted me here."

"Come in then, young man. If you don't know very much, you have certainly come to the right place. You look very intelligent to me. I'd wager that you will be an out-standing student."

"Thank you, sir. Please, should I sit at the front?"

"Yes, Timothy, at the front." The boys had stacked their wood beside the fireplace, and Nathan added two pieces to the blaze before he turned to the waiting room.

He told them a little about himself, that he grew up in Coventry, about thirty miles away, and that he had seven brothers and two sisters. "The two youngest are David and Joanna. They are thirteen and ten years of age. I fancy they are like many of you in their interests and pleasures." He did not mention his stepsister. At one time he would have included her as one of his sisters, but of late this had changed. He told them that he had studied at Yale College and had graduated there. He told them that Union School was not his first teaching job. He told them he liked being a schoolmaster and that there was nothing he would rather do than teach. He paused in his speech then, and for a quiet moment he looked from face to face. "Do you have any questions? Is there anything you want to ask me?"

A boy near the back put his hand up, then stood. "I have a question, sir," he said. "Do you drink English tea?"

A small murmur rose from the group, but Nathan held up his hand to quiet them. "John has a question." He took a step down the center aisle between the tables and stopped to look at the questioner. "I am correct, am I not? Your name is John?"

"Yes, sir, John Carver."

"Well, John, I will tell you. I drink sassafras tea. I drink raspberry tea. I even drink sage tea. I drink liberty tea only."

"Sir," said a boy who sat in the middle of the bench across the room, "my name is Thomas Allen. May I speak?"

"Yes, Thomas."

The boy slid his legs one at a time over the back of the bench and stood. "You support what they did in Boston, then, do you, sir?"

"I don't honestly know, Thomas. I don't know what I would have done had I been in Boston, but I do know I will not drink tea from England. I will not support taxes levied against us by a parliament in which we do not have a representative."

"But, sir, doesn't the king rule us because God gave him that right? That's what my grandfather says."

Nathan waited a minute before he spoke. What should

he say to this boy? It was not his job to diminish the boy's respect for his grandfather. "I have told you what I believe, Thomas, but let me stress that each man must think for himself. Your grandfather's thinking is different from mine. We won't use our school time to argue about the rebellion. There will be no more discussion on the subject. We none of us here are enemies."

"But, sir, you and my grandfather will be enemies if it comes to war."

"No one wants war." Nathan sighed deeply. He knew his words were not totally true. Some young men would welcome being part of a battle, but he was not one of those men. "Let us all pray there will be no fighting." A small shudder passed through him. The idea of shooting at anyone, especially at a fellow Englishman or maybe even a man from Connecticut, made him feel sick. "Let us begin our studies," he said.

And so Nathan Hale turned away the thoughts of war. He thought only about letters and about words and about ideas. He kept the fire blazing high, and the room was warm. He learned each boy's name, and they learned that his spirit was gentle, his smile quick. Before that first day was over, they were comfortable with one another and glad to be in that schoolroom together.

When the last scholar was gone, Nathan banked the fire and locked the door. He drew his coat close against the sharp March wind and followed the path down the hill that stood at the edge of town. After a short walk, he turned on the street that led to the Lawrence home. He felt lucky to be boarding in the stately white home with one of the most prosperous families in town. He opened the gate of the fence that surrounded the front garden and stood, looking up for a minute at the bottom of the wide front steps.

This was the home of Mr. William Lawrence, a banker and one of the school proprietors. It was a good place to live. Of course, living under the constant observation of one of the men who paid your salary could have some disadvantages, especially when that man had a lovely young niece who also lived with him.

Betsy Lawrence had the most beautiful hair Nathan had ever seen. He loved the way those golden curls escaped from the ribbon that held them up and then tumbled down the young lady's soft cheek. Her face was charming too, laughing blue eyes and a sweetly turned-up mouth. "*Whoa,*" he said aloud to himself. "You can't start thinking about the lady all the time." Before coming to New London, he had felt fairly certain that he would eventually ask his stepsister to marry him, but now he was not so sure.

He started up the steps. No, he would wait, and he would certainly not get involved with Betsy Lawrence. If he paid her any attention, she might want to get married. Nathan was not ready for marriage. His job was not secure enough, not yet. Besides, he was thinking of joining the New London militia. A wife might not approve of his being a man who promised to bear arms. If he became entwined with the niece of his employer, there could be all kinds of problems. He opened the ornately carved front door and climbed the polished front stairs to go to his room.

Someone, a servant no doubt, had built a fire in the room's fireplace. He pulled a chair close and read the letter that had been placed on his bed. His father wrote of the farm, of the family, and finally of political problems. "There's trouble blowing in from across the sea," Deacon Hale wrote. "It is bound to rage hard against us."

He had only just finished the letter when a knock sounded on his door. "Momma says you are to come to the table now," called a boy's voice.

Nathan took his watch from his pocket. He had been told the family ate at six, and the time was only five thirty. He hurried from his room to follow Robert down the stairs.

The others were already at the table. "Forgive me, kind lady," Nathan said to Mistress Lawrence, who sat at one end of the table.

She smiled at him. "Not at all, Master Hale. The meal is early tonight. Mister Lawrence has a meeting to attend."

"Yes," said her husband from the other end of the table. "The monthly meeting of the school proprietors." He smiled. "I've already heard a glowing report of your first day from my boys."

Robert slid into the seat beside his brother, Isaiah, leaving Nathan to sit across the table beside Miss Betsy. This was Nathan's third meal with the family, and each time the place beside Betsy was his. He was afraid the seating assignment was permanent. He was also afraid that sitting near a lady so beautiful would make him unable to carry on a sensible conversation.

He did manage "Thank you, sir" to Mr. Lawrence and a smile at the two boys. He collected his thoughts and went on. "I believe my scholars and I will get along very well." He filled his plate with food that was passed to him. Last came a bowl of cooked apples. As he dipped in the spoon, Nathan remembered Jonah, and he told Mr. Lawrence about the boy. "I fervently wish to see the boy's education continue." He shrugged. "He says, though, that his father will not allow him to accept charity."

Mistress Lawrence made a sort of clucking sound with her tongue. "Poor boy, and him with no mother. His sister, Mercy, is a dear child too."

"Really she's not a child, Auntie," said Betsy. "I believe Mercy is my age. At sixteen she is certainly old enough for marriage, and she's a beauty. I wonder that some man hasn't claimed her for his wife."

"Would that such a marriage might occur and thus solve a mountain of problems for Mercy and the boy after their father is gone." Mistress Lawrence cocked her head, thinking. "William, perhaps you could speak to Richard Tyler. You know he lost his wife last year, and he has three small children to care for."

"Auntie," said Betsy, "I hardly think Mercy Hawkins would want you to arrange a marriage for her. Mister Richard Tyler does not even wash his hands when he comes to meeting."

Mr. Lawrence held up a hand to quiet his niece. "Don't

fret yourself, girl. I won't be holding forth with Richard Tyler on the subject of marriage." He turned to Nathan. "I've little doubt your cousin Samuel will see to the children when poor Patrick Hawkins is buried. Most likely he will send them to New Haven. There's an orphanage there that will keep Jonah until he's fourteen, and likely Mercy can work for her keep."

"Why will it be Samuel's responsibility?" Nathan asked.

"Hawkins worked for Mister Reynolds, sailed on a whaling boat for years, then came to shore, married him a wife, and stayed in New London to work in the mill. I'll say your cousin handles the people who work for him more kindly than his father-in-law did. He's been much appreciated in this town." He shook his head. "Likely he will ruin that, though, spouting his Tory notions. Old Josh Reynolds is likely turning in his grave, a Tory living in his fine home."

"Please, Mister Lawrence," his wife said, and leaned forward in her chair. "Let's not get into politics at the table. We could all end up with indigestion."

"Master Hale doesn't drink English tea," Isaiah blurted out.

"Isaiah, really!" said his mother.

"Well, he doesn't! Isn't that so, Robert?"

"I did tell the boys that today, madam," Nathan said, "but I also told them we would not argue about taxes or rebellion while we should be at lessons."

"It's glad I am that you don't want English tea, Mr.

Hale," said William Lawrence, giving his wife a small smile. "Because you'd be hard-pressed to find such a drink in this house, and that's all I'll say on the subject for tonight." He turned to his wife. "Outstanding roast beef, Mistress Lawrence, outstanding!"

After the meal was finished, Nathan set out for a visit with his cousin. He went first to the Lawrence stable to get his horse. The estate that had been built by Joshua Reynolds lay a mile or so out and on the other side of town. A gray stone mansion stood on a rise at the end of a long driveway. Nathan had visited his cousin two days earlier, when he had first arrived in New London. He had been surprised then by the luxury, but at night the house looked even more magnificent, like a castle with lights blazing. Nathan stood looking up. He doubted if any other member of his family had ever lived in such splendor, with servants everywhere to do their bidding and thick, soft carpet to walk on.

Nathan had not grown up poor. With four hundred acres of land on which to grow crops and graze cattle, Nathan's father had been a man of means in Coventry. The Hale home was large, housing a big family, but nothing like this palace Samuel lived in. Nathan knew his father's Puritan background would not let him approve of living so lavishly. He shrugged and began to climb the stone steps that led from the road up to the door. To each his own. Samuel was different from Nathan, and not only in his thinking about the rebellion.

The knock was answered by a butler. "Do come in,

sir," said the man whom he had met on his previous visit. "You may wait for Mister Hale in the library, if you please. There's a big warm fire going there."

"Thank you. A fire sounds appealing." Nathan followed the servant, who opened the library door with a flourishing gesture. "I'll just let Mister Hale know you are here."

One wall of the room was covered with bookcases made of rich dark wood. Nathan moved immediately and began to read the titles of the volumes. There were plays by Shakespeare, volumes of poetry and history. He touched the book spines gently, almost caressingly. Once Nathan might have congratulated himself with the number of books he had worked to possess, but his collection was nothing compared to this. Would his cousin lend him books? What a joy it would be to share even parts of these great works with his students. He spotted a favorite, *Cato*, a play by Joseph Addison. He slipped the volume from the shelf, opened it to his favorite part, and began to read. The man Cato stood over the dead body of his son, Marcus.

Just then the library door opened and Samuel came in. After the two men exchanged greetings, Nathan said, "I've just been looking at what Cato said when the body of his son is brought to him. I've always loved those words."

"Ah, yes." Samuel nodded his head. "Read me the passage."

" 'How beautiful is death when earned by virtue. Who would not be that youth! What pity is it that we can die but once to serve our country.' "

Nathan looked up at Samuel, who had closed his eyes during the reading. "I would die for England, Nathan," said Samuel. "England would be worth it." He paused for a minute and put his hand on Nathan's shoulder. "But not this foolish rebellion. Surely you would not give up your life for such nonsense."

A fiery anger came up from inside Nathan. He wanted to shout that liberty could not be called nonsense, but he checked himself. He was a visitor in his cousin's home. He had come here to ask for help, help much needed by the boy Jonah. He would not argue about politics, not tonight. He forced a laugh. "Let's not talk of dying, Cousin. I don't believe things will go that far. Surely we are all reasonable men."

Samuel laughed too. "Just so, just so. Forgive me. I do get carried away at times. My Jayne tells me I am often too zealous." He motioned Nathan toward a chair near the fire. "Sit down, and let us have a conversation with no mention of that subject on which we are so quick to disagree. Jayne will be sorry to have missed you. She's taken little Tobias and gone to Boston to visit friends and do a bit of shopping."

"I am sorry to have missed your wife. Please give her my regards." Nathan looked for a moment into the fire, then went on. "I came to ask your advice and mayhap your assistance."

"Ask," said his cousin. "I should be proud to help you in any way possible."

"It's about the boy Jonah Hawkins. He wants to go to

school, but there is no money because of his father's illness. I've thought of endeavoring to pay his way myself, although to be honest it would be hard on my beginning wage. Jonah, though, says his father would never allow the family to accept charity."

Samuel pursed his lips, thinking. "Old Patrick is proud, but I think his love for his children might outweigh his pride. He came to fatherhood late in life, after a life at sea on one of the whalers owned by my father-in-law. He does dote on that girl and boy." Samuel nodded his head. "Young Master Hawkins will be among your scholars, not tomorrow, but soon. I'll have a bit of conversation with the father and see to it that the family is not left wanting."

"Jonah is afraid his father won't live long," Nathan said.

"He may well be correct. I think the old fellow's heart may be worn out. It is not an easy life he's had. If he dies, a place will need be found for the two of them. When it comes to that, I'll see to the details myself."

Nathan thought of requesting that Jonah not be sent away to an orphans' asylum, but he thought it best not to bring up anything more right then. He and Samuel spent some time discussing the Union School, life in New London, and their cousins in Massachusetts. They bantered about their colleges, Samuel making jokes about Nathan's Yale, and Nathan handing them back about Samuel's Harvard.

Standing at the door, saying good-bye, Nathan felt a warmth toward his cousin that he had feared might not be there. Samuel Hale might have misdirected loyalty to the king of England, but Nathan could see that the bond of blood between them would hold.

"Come again soon, Cousin," Samuel said. "Come and read, come and take books back with you. Wait just a minute." He turned and disappeared into the house, returning with *Cato*. "Take this with you. It's yours." He pressed the book into Nathan's palm.

Outside, with the book held tightly in his hand, Nathan mounted his horse, and at first he urged the animal to move quickly, but soon he slowed and listened to the sounds of the horse's shoes on the cobblestones of the driveway. From near the water came the cry of a bird, possibly an early loon? The birds were beginning to come back. Soon it would be spring.

He looked up at the stars, the same stars that had shone over his home in Coventry. On summer evenings he often lay with his brothers in the grass and stared up at the stars. Nathan was suddenly unbearably homesick.

CHAPTER THREE

The Boy

Jonah Hawkins looked at the stars that night too, and he too felt lonely. He walked back toward the small cottage from the well. He set down his bucket and studied the sky. How many stars were there? He wondered if anyone knew. He would ask Master Hale if ever he had the chance.

Tomorrow his father and Mercy were supposed to be home. He was glad. He did not like to live in the quiet house alone. Mercy always sang as she went about her work, and the one good thing about his father's illness was that he stayed most often in a chair beside the fire, always ready to tell stories of his days on the big whaling ships. Jonah picked up the water pail, took one more look at the stars, and moved toward the back door.

His father and sister did return the next day. Mercy fixed a good supper of sweet potatoes with a bit of salted pork, and Jonah thanked her for it when they had finished eating.

"Well," she said, "having no one to cook for you seems to have improved your manners, I'd say."

Jonah stoked the fire and was about to settle on the floor near his father's feet, when the knock at the door came. Jonah did not want company. He had planned to ask his father to tell the story about the time a great whale bumped the ship again and again, almost spilling men and equipment into the dark sea.

Mercy went to the door. "Come in, Master Hale, sir," she said, and Jonah thought Master Hale had come to talk to his father about allowing him to attend school. He sighed, knowing the teacher was wasting his time, but even before his sister stepped aside to admit the visitor, Jonah had realized he was wrong. Mercy did not know the teacher. Yet she had not hesitated to say "Master Hale."

It was Mr. Samuel Hale who stepped into their home. Jonah scrambled quickly to his feet. His father's employer had never visited them before. The man looked odd in their small cottage. He was tall and broad of shoulders, filling the doorway as he stepped inside. His fine clothing looked out of place among the simple surroundings of the spinning wheel, rough wood table, and hasty pudding cooking over the fire.

Mr. Hale held out his hand in protest when Jonah's father started to rise from his chair. "Don't get up, Patrick," he said.

Mercy hurried to move their other chair close to the fire. Jonah stood awkwardly beside his father, but his sister motioned that he should come sit at the bench beside the table. Something important was about to happen, and Jonah perched on the edge of his seat while his father and Mr. Hale exchanged the pleasantries of a beginning conversation. They commented on the weather, and Mr. Hale asked about the older man's health.

Jonah knew their visitor had come to discuss some definite subject, but he was surprised when that subject turned out to be himself. "I'd like to talk to you about your son," Mr. Hale said. Jonah started to rise, but Mercy, sitting beside him, put out her hand to stay him.

"What is it you have to say about my Jonah?" his father asked, and Jonah thought his father's voice had a bit of unease in it. Did he think Jonah had made some sort of trouble in town?

"My kinsman is the new schoolmaster, Nathan Hale, by name. He tells me that he met your son and thought him to be an intelligent lad. My cousin would like to have the boy in school, and I would like to make that possible." Jonah could not sit still and listen. Despite his sister's hand, he stood up and crept as quietly as possible to the door.

Outside he ran, first down the lane, but then he came back to go to the cow shed. He had not bothered to take a coat, and he was shaking when Mercy came, her shawl drawn tight, to find him. "Foolish boy," she said. "Why are you shivering here? Did you not want to hear what was said about you?"

"I couldn't," he said. "Too much rose up in me."

She reached for his hand and pulled him from the shed's corner. "You do want schooling, do you not?"

"More than anything," he said, his teeth chattering.

"Well then, back inside with you. Your benefactor is about to leave, and you needs thank him."

"Oh, I do. I do, indeed." A great excitement rushed through Jonah's body, and he felt warm.

Mr. Samuel Hale had already left the cottage, and his driver had climbed down to open the coach door. Jonah raced to call, "Sir, I want to say thank you. I thank you with all of my heart."

The man stepped close to him, and he put his hand on Jonah's shoulder. In the moonlight, Jonah could see his kind eyes. "You are most welcome, my boy. Now you must work hard and make us all proud."

"Oh, I will, sir. I'll work harder than any boy ever has before." Jonah moved back to stand beside his sister. They watched as Mr. Hale got up into the coach. The driver urged the horse onto the lane.

"What a fine man he is!" said Mercy. "Father agreed at once. How could it be otherwise with a splendid man as Mister Samuel Hale wanting to see you educated?"

Inside the cottage, their father had already made his way to bed. Jonah knelt on the floor, his head resting on his father's cover. "I'm grateful," he said, "grateful to you and to Mister Hale."

"Don't forget to be grateful to God too, boy," said his father. "Mayhap you will grow up to be a gentleman like Mister Hale. You'll make a man would have made your mother proud."

"The new schoolmaster lost his mother when he was

young too," said Jonah. "He's a good teacher, Father, but he says he won't drink English tea." He stopped, and fought the urge to clap a hand over his mouth. Why had he said that?

His father pushed himself up in the bed. "That's drivel! It's a surprise, a kinsman of Mister Hale's speaking so." He frowned and shook his head. "Mayhap I made a hasty decision, agreeing to send you to such a man, paid for or no."

Jonah straightened himself, his words tumbling out. "Oh no, Father, Master Hale says we won't use schooltime to fight the rebellion. He says each man must decide for himself which side is right."

"Right?" shouted his father. "I'll tell you what's right. It's right for the people of Connecticut to act like Englishmen. We've always been Englishmen, and Englishmen bow to the king."

Jonah wanted to cut out his tongue. Why had he mentioned the tea? He knew how his father felt about the rebellion. Excitement had loosened his tongue. He jumped to his feet. "But you won't stay me from school? Tell me so, please."

The old man lay back on the pillow. "Mister Samuel Hale thinks you should go. I'll trust in his judgment." He put up his hand to hold to Jonah's arm. "But you must swear never to listen to the man spout treason."

"I'll think for myself, Father. I promise." Later, when Jonah lay on his own cot, he thought back over the conversation. He had vowed to think for himself. His father had not noticed his choice of words, had been satisfied that his son would always be a loyal subject to the king. Jonah stared out into the night. Mayhap he would never have to decide. He was only twelve years old. He would work hard just as he had told Mr. Hale, and he would keep quiet. He might just decide not to join either side. None of it really mattered to him, only just a scrawny boy.

The next morning, Mercy made him a lunch of bread and leftover salted pork. The weather was warmer, and Jonah enjoyed the walk to school. His path lay along the side of the Thames River. He turned his gaze downward. Before long the grass at the water's edge would begin to turn green. He would not miss the first signs of spring because every day he would go to school. "School!" he shouted to the bare trees. "I'm going to school!" He began to sing.

> *The lookout in the crosstrees, stood,*
> *With spyglass in his hand;*
> *There's a whale, there's a whale,*
> *And a whalefish he cried,*
> *And she blows at every span, brave boys,*
> *She blows at every span.*
> *Our harpoon struck and the line played out,*
> *With a single flourish of his tail,*
> *He capsized the boat and we lost five men,*
> *And we did not catch the wale, brave boys,*
> *And we did not catch the whale.*

He sang until he could see the building. Two large wooden barrels stood in the school yard. Several students and Master Hale were standing around them. Jonah hurried closer and heard Master Hale say, "Not now. You'll have to wait until you've all done your part."

While they filed into the building, Jonah had a chance for a quick question about the barrels. "Claims he can jump from inside one to inside another." Thomas shrugged his shoulders. "Don't know as I believe him."

Jonah looked at the man who stood in front of the schoolroom. He was the man who had made it possible for Jonah to come to this building to learn. He was the man whose smile and pat on the back had greeted him. Jonah nodded his head. "I do," he whispered. "If Master Hale said he could jump, by Jove, he'll jump." For a moment he tried to picture the stern Master Tracy jumping from a barrel. He smiled. Union School would be different this term.

The scholars fell quickly to their work, but the boy waited for his chance. It came when the teacher appeared to examine Jonah's Latin copybook. "Please, sir," he said, careful to keep his voice low, "may I know about the barrels?"

"It's only a bit of fun, a promise I'll jump from one to the other when all my Latin pupils can conjugate the assigned verbs and all the beginning English students can recite the first-primer rhymes." He smiled at Jonah and pointed to the copybook. "Now, it's back to work with you."

At noontime, Jonah opened the cloth that wrapped his meal. Holding meat in one hand and bread in the other, he ate as quickly as possible. The teacher had declared that in celebration of the first warm day there would be time for a quick game or two.

Outside he joined a group of others already organizing races. "I want to race you." John Carver reached out to grab at Thomas Allen's arm.

Thomas shook his head. "Don't feel like running today." He jerked his arm free and turned away.

"But you won last time," John said, and moved quickly to step in Thomas's path. "I wager I'll best you today."

"Not interested." Thomas started to walk away.

"You're afraid," yelled John.

Thomas stopped walking and turned back. "I am not afraid," he said.

John snarled. "Your father is afraid and so is your grandfather. That's why they're loyal to the king."

Thomas's face turned red. "That is an untruth! We are loyalists because we are true Englishmen. People who are not loyal to the king will hang. Do you want to hang, John?"

"Coward!" jeered John, and he pushed Thomas. In an instant the boys were rolling on the ground, landing blows on each other when they could. The other boys made a circle around them.

"Get the dirty Tory," one of the watchers called, and others began to shout encouragement to one or the other of the fighters.

"Stop that!" The teacher's voice was loud. "Stop it at once!"

Jonah whirled to see Master Hale run down the steps. The crowd of boys parted to let the teacher through.

Master Hale reached down to grab a boy's shirt with each hand. "We will have no more brawling." He jerked the boys to sitting positions, then let them go. "Inside!" he shouted. "Both of you, immediately."

The group of watchers stood frozen. The boys got to their feet, but when they began to dust themselves off, the teacher took hold of them again. "Now," he said.

When the door closed behind the teacher, one of the boys said softly, "He'll whip the dickens out of them now."

"Like as not, he'll strip them of their shirts and lash their backs," said another.

"No," said Jonah. "I daresay he won't strike them at all." He looked at the building.

"Stop talking," someone said. "I want to hear should they cry out."

They stood about waiting, and Jonah bit at his lip. Shortly, Master Hale came out the door and rang a small bell. The boys filed in silently. Inside, Jonah looked around for the offenders. "Take your places," the teacher said, and eyes down, the scholars found their spots.

Master Hale walked down the center aisle and stood in front of his desk. Jonah noticed that in one hand the teacher held a heavy ruler. Had he used that ruler to punish John and Thomas? Jonah's heart beat quickly. Master Hale had told him there would be no physical punishments in his school. Where were the culprits? A hunk of bread still lay unfinished on the table where John had left it. Across the aisle Thomas's spot too was empty.

"I will not tolerate unruly behavior," said Master Hale.

"I most certainly will not tolerate conflicts because one boy upholds the actions of Parliament and another one does not. Our world is full of chaos, but in Union School we will have peace." He folded his arms across his chest. "Young Master Allen and young Master Carver are upstairs." He pointed toward the ceiling. "They will do lessons up there until they can behave in a civilized manner. Here there will be no loyalists, no rebels. There will be only scholars and a teacher."

Like most of the other boys, Jonah turned to look at the stairs. They had never climbed the narrow steps to the attic room. Master Tracy had kept personal belongings up there and had forbidden student entry.

Jonah smiled. His former teacher would have beaten the boys for fighting. Master Hale had said he did not believe in physical punishment. Jonah liked this teacher's ideas. Then he remembered that his father called Master Hale's ideas treason. The boy hoped his teacher would not be punished by the king.

For a month, Jonah walked to school, watching for signs of spring on his path, and then suddenly green began to appear on the tree limbs and in spots of grass. Slowly birds came back too, and finally one night he heard the sound for which he waited. He had gone to the woodlot for firewood and arms full, had just managed to open the door when he heard the call of the loon. He paused, listening, one foot inside the cottage, loving the haunting, eerie cry. His father said likely the two black-headed birds were the same pair, returning each year, and Jonah wondered where they had traveled for the winter. What faraway places had those birds seen?

On the third Saturday of April, Jonah declared it was officially spring, and he hurried through his chores. Taking some bread and cheese, he told Mercy not to hold supper for him, and he wandered down the path all the way to where the river joined the ocean. Long Island Sound they called that special place where river and ocean came together. He found a rock for sitting and settled beside the water with his knees bent up, arms wrapped around them.

Jonah loved the sounds of the waves hitting against the shore. He had come here often with his father, who also loved it. "The sea's in your blood, boy." His father's words came to his mind as clearly as if they had just been spoken. It was true, but Jonah had no wish to be a sailor. He yearned too much for books to find a sailor's life appealing. Would he mayhap study law? Or could he be a teacher, like Master Hale?

After a time he took out his bread and cheese, and he ate it with a bit of guilt while watching the gulls search for food. When he finished, he bent to put his hand into the cold water and felt the force of it beat against his skin. No, he wouldn't sail the ocean as a sailor. He would never live far from the sea, though, and he hoped to cross this vast water someday. His father had come from England with his parents as a small boy, and he told tales of his homeland.

Jonah would like to visit London Town, although he knew he would never love it as he did New London. Even his father admitted to liking the weather in his new home better. London, he had told Jonah, was too often rainy and dreary. Still, Jonah wanted to see the place. Maybe he would catch a glimpse of George III riding out of the palace gates to go about royal business.

Would the crown on the king's head shine brighter than the sun? But then, maybe the king did not wear his crown when he went out of the castle. If he saw the king, would he bow or stand stock-still? His father, he knew, would want him to bow, but he wondered if Master Hale would. His teacher stuck to his policy of not discussing the rebellion, and there had been no more fights.

Still, there was no real peace at Union School. Jonah could feel most of the boys beginning to pull away from the few who were loyalists. He desired to be in neither camp. He only wanted the troublesome business to be done with. He wanted peace in Connecticut. He should go home. Reluctantly, he stood and started the return journey.

Mercy ran to meet him on the lane. "I've watched for you, watched for more than a while." She pushed back the dark hair that had fallen into her face. "Father's taken a turn for the worse. I fetched Doctor Wade, but he says there's nothing more to be done." She paused and closed her eyes for a moment. Then she opened them and put her hand on his arm. "Jonah, he says Father likely won't last the night."

He broke from her then, running at full speed. "Wait, Jonah, wait," she called, and he did. "He's asleep now. What's to be gained by you busting in to wake him?"

Jonah wiped at the tears that pushed from his eyes. "What will it be like? What's our life without Father?"

"I've no answer to your questions, Brother, but we stay together. I promise that much. Somehow, we stay together."

Jonah kicked at pebbles on the road. "There's Aunt Mary. Do you think she'd have us?"

Mercy let her breath go in a long sigh. "She's old, older than Father even. She told me when we tarried there that she'd not be able to keep up the rent. She's likely vacated already and gone to her daughter's in Norwich." She shook her head. "There'd be no place for us with Cousin Sally, her with six young ones of her own."

The boy swallowed, fighting sobs. "Father had the rent paid. He told me so when he said I'd have to stay out of school this term. We can just stay where we are, at least for a time."

Mercy frowned. "Another payment is due come June. Doubtless, we will be turned out then even if Father still lives. I fear it's the workhouse for us, but we'll make do, Jonah, and we will stay together."

They moved quietly into the cottage. Mercy took the chair beside their father's bed, and Jonah settled on the floor. From time to time, Mercy wiped her father's face with a wet cloth, and she put drops of water from a spoon into his mouth.

Sometime in the darkest part of the night, the old man spoke. "Jonah," he murmured. "Jonah."

Jonah had fallen asleep, his head resting against the bed, but he was awake and off the floor in an instant. Leaning over the bed, he took his father's hand. "What is it, Father? I'm here."

"Jonah, my boy." The dry whisper seemed to echo against the dark walls. "Jonah, be careful of the whale. Promise me to be mindful of the whale."

Jonah was mystified. Was his father thinking of the Bible story where a man with Jonah's name was swallowed by a whale, or did he think himself back on a ship, struggling with a mighty creature? It mattered not. His father only wanted assurance that his son would be careful. "I will, Father. I'll be watchful of the whale, always."

"Mercy," their father said. "It's a good girl you are, and one to make me proud. Keep your brother from the whale. He is needful of your help."

"I will, Father." Mercy swallowed a sob. "I'll keep Jonah from the whale."

Their father closed his eyes and said no more. Any need of sleep was gone from Jonah. He passed the rest of the night near the window, staring out at the stars. Just before day, a strange sort of rattling sound came from his father, and then the room was quiet. Mercy leaned forward to put her hand on their father's chest. Jonah knew even before his sister spoke. "He's gone," she said. "Our father is with us no more."

CHAPTER FOUR

The Man

Spending time with Miss Betsy Lawrence was not part of Nathan Hale's plan that spring Saturday. Right after breakfast, he decided to go fishing. Mister Lawrence still lingered at the table with his tea and newspapers when Nathan came to ask advice about a good spot.

His landlord looked up from his reading. "Oh," he said, "there's a fine spot not more than a mile from here. Just go two blocks over to Water Street, and down to the river. There's a big log there to the north a bit, splendid location. Popular, though. You'd best make haste before someone takes the place."

Mistress Lawrence turned from the table where she stacked dishes and she smiled. "Should we count on fish for our evening meal, then?" she asked.

"I'm afraid not." He grimaced. "I'm taking a book too. Often I forget to heed my line and let the fish escape."

Betsy came out from the kitchen, a dish towel in her

hand. "Don't worry," she said. "I'll make my special stew, just in case."

He whistled as he walked, his book under one arm, his pole over his shoulder, and a pail in one hand. He liked New London and its wonderful Thames River, liked the way the people of New London pronounced the name of their river differently from the way the people of London, England, pronounced theirs with the same spelling. "Here we call it Thames, the way it is spelled, not 'Tims' like they do over there," he had written recently to one of his Yale friends. "The Thames is America's version, simple and straightforward."

At the riverbank, the grass was green and inviting. He scrambled down the incline, pleased to see no one had beaten him to the log. In fact, there was no other fisherman in sight, and Nathan liked that. He did not feel like company. He baited his hook with the bits of pork taken from breakfast leftovers, filled his pail with water, and settled on the log. The morning sun felt good, and his spirits were high. Because he had read *The Canterbury Tales* before, he was able to keep a part of his mind on the pole, and by late morning his pail held six fish. Betsy's stew could be saved for another day.

Nathan looked up at the sun, almost overhead. Likely he should start back in order to have time to wash up before the noontide meal. He glanced down at his book. No, it wouldn't take long to finish "The Cook's Tale." He had just begun to read again when he heard someone call, "Nathan, oh, Nathan."

Betsy Lawrence inched her way down the bank. She

carried a large basket, but still she managed to wave at him. *I don't want company*, he thought, but he did not turn away. She was decidedly the most beautiful girl he'd ever seen. The thought had crossed his mind before, but now there was no denying it. Wisps of her magnificent hair stuck out from beneath her bonnet to appear even more golden in the sunlight. Her blue dress, one he had never seen, fit her in just the right way to emphasize the curves of her body. He threw down his pole and ran to meet her. "Let me take the basket!" he shouted.

"I've brought us a picnic," she said when he was beside her, and all resentment at having his solitude interrupted drained from him.

Betsy took a cloth from the top of the basket and spread it on the ground in front of the log. Then she laid out buttered bread, sliced ham, apples, and small tea cakes. "It looks wonderful," Nathan said, but he was thinking how wonderful she looked.

They settled themselves on the cloth and leaned against the log. "It's a lovely day, isn't it?" she asked when the food was all passed out.

He looked up from his ham. "Yes, lovely. You are lovely. I mean . . ." His face turned red. "I meant to say the day is lovely, but"—he shrugged—"obviously, I said what I was really thinking. I hope you don't mind."

She smiled at him, her blue eyes shining. "Of course I don't mind. I fear it is I who have been forward, coming here this way uninvited, but we never have any time to talk, just the two of us."

Nathan could have told her that he had been careful to make sure they were never alone, but the thought only briefly played at the edge of his mind. He could not have, at the moment, explained why he had thought it wise to keep a distance between himself and the lady.

They talked about his school, and he told her his plan to act on his belief that girls should be just as educated as boys. "You're a strange man, Nathan Hale," she said, her tone teasing. "Strange, but very interesting."

"So," he said, "do you not yearn for more education?"

She cocked her head and looked at him for a long moment. She did not smile, but her eyes danced with merriment. "Before I answer, you must supply more information."

"More information?" He leaned toward her.

"Yes, I must know who my teacher would be should I desire more education." She laughed.

"Would it not be enough to say you would have a good teacher?" He could feel his heart racing.

She gave her head a strong shake. "Oh no," she said. "Before I should desire more education I would need a handsome and charming schoolmaster. In fact, I would need Nathan Hale himself." She leaned in his direction and for a moment he imagined that their lips might touch, but then she jumped up. Look!" She pointed toward a small boat moored a few yards away. "Let's go for a ride!"

He stood up in order to see better. "But whose bateau is it?"

"It belongs to Mister Harrison, I believe, but everyone

uses it and leaves it somewhere along the bank." She began to gather the picnic remains. She shook the cloth, then began to fold it. "What does *bateau* mean?"

"It's a French word for that kind of boat, flat bottom, pointed ends. I believe it actually means boat."

"See!" She reached for the basket. "I need just such a teacher as you!" She took a couple of steps, then turned back to motion to him. "Come on! I want a ride on a bateau!"

He hesitated for a moment, then picked up his pole and pail. "If we aren't coming back here, I'll need to take my fish."

"Now," she said when she had settled in one end of the small boat with him at the other end rowing, "this is pleasant, isn't it?"

He laughed. "Little wonder you find it pleasant. I am doing all the work!"

"But I could do it," she said with mock indignation. "I wonder, though, if you really wish to be seen traveling the Thames with a lady manning the oars."

They had just gone around a bend when Nathan spotted a man on the bank. "Betsy!" He shouted, and he waved. "They told me I might find you down here."

Nathan began to turn the boat to shore. "It's Lyman Wolcott," Betsy said under her breath. "I'd just as soon he hadn't found us."

There was no preventing the meeting, though, because the boat was already against the bank, and without waiting to be invited, Lyman Wolcott was climbing aboard.

Betsy introduced the two men. "Hale?" said Lyman. "Are you a relation of Samuel Hale's?" Something in the man's tone did not sit well with Nathan.

"Samuel is my cousin," he said, and he met Lyman's gaze directly until the man dropped his eyes.

"So I suppose you are a Tory too?" His voice held contempt and he almost spat the question.

Nathan had stood to be introduced to Lyman, but now he took his time settling back onto the bottom of the boat. His hand was on the rough wood, and a sliver broke away and pierced his skin. The splinter, though, was less irritating than Lyman Wolcott's question and his accompanying sneer. Nathan spoke slowly. "My cousin and I do not hold the same political views, yet I feel a great deal of respect and affection for Samuel."

Lyman made a sort of huffing sound. "Really? I'd rethink that respect and affection were I you!"

Don't let him get to you, Nathan told himself. He's like the boys you teach, wanting to fight in the school yard. "I have no intention of turning my back on my kinsman just because we are on different sides of a disagreement. Samuel is a fine man."

"Disagreement?" Lyman laughed, and the sound was derisive. "*Disagreement* is a mild word for war, don't you think?" He shifted his weight, and the toe of his boot poked slightly into Nathan's leg.

Was it an accident? Before the answer had time to form in his mind, Nathan was up and standing almost nose to nose with Lyman.

Betsy too got quickly to her feet. "Gentlemen . . ." There was no time for her to say more. The quick movement rocked the boat that had drifted unnoticed away from the bank to be caught by a swift undercurrent. The boat swayed, and the three occupants were thrown to one side. Suddenly the boat was turning over.

Nathan felt himself go under the water. When he popped back up, his eyes searched the surface. "Betsy?" he called. Then he saw her. She clung to the upturned boat, and she had been carried to the middle of the river. "Hold on!" he yelled. "I'll come to you." Just then Lyman too came to the surface, and he grabbed for Nathan, fastening himself to Nathan's neck and pushing him back under the water, himself going under too. *He's going to drown himself and me with him*, Nathan thought, and he fought to free himself. With one mighty surge of strength, he pushed the other man away from him.

Lyman disappeared under the water. Frantic, Nathan looked about and spotted a large tree limb floating nearby. He swam for the limb. Then, holding it with one hand, he made his way back to where he had seen Lyman go under. He let go the limb and dove under the water, searching. His hand touched something, a body. He pulled, fighting the force of the water that wanted to hold him under. Gasping for breath, he broke the surface, grabbed the branch, and thrust Lyman away from himself and toward the branch. "There," he yelled, "hold on to the limb."

For a second, Nathan thought the man would go under again, but spitting and coughing, Lyman reached for the branch. Nathan left him then and swam toward the boat and Betsy. "You were wonderful," she said when he was beside her.

"Wanted to let him drown," he said. He began to swim toward the bank, holding the small boat with one hand. "Kick," he told Betsy. "Even ladies have to help this time."

Nathan swam, and he watched Lyman float to the water's edge and climb out. He swam some more and finally pulled the boat with Betsy still clinging to it to the bank. Lyman sat up from where he had stretched himself on the grass. He reached out his hand to pull Betsy up onto the land; then he turned to Nathan. "Thank you, Hale, . . . for the help out there, I mean," he said, but Nathan saw the darkness in the man's eyes and thought the gratitude was given grudgingly. Lyman turned back to Betsy. "Betsy, you poor thing," he said, "you must be freezing. I'll see you home at once."

Nathan reached out to take Betsy's arm. "I'll get Miss Lawrence home," he said, and without waiting for a reply, they began to move up the hill.

"One moment, here," Lyman called. "Is that what you want, Betsy, or would you rather I took you?"

Betsy did not even look back. "I'll go with Nathan," she called. "He boards with us."

"Even so, I rather think . . . ," said Lyman, but his words trailed off.

"I'll get you a blanket," said Nathan when they had climbed up to the street. "Wait here." She stood on the walk while he went to the door of the first home they came to, to explain their plight.

They were given blankets and a ride home. "I'm so sorry. I caused the upset when I jumped up," said Betsy when they were settled on the carriage seat.

"It was my fault for getting up in the first place. I let the man's words push me to anger." He frowned. "I behaved no better than a schoolboy."

"Lyman was unpleasant. It made him angry, I think, to see us together." She pulled her blanket closer around her. "I've told him before that I didn't want to be courted by him, but he doesn't seem to believe me."

"Well, I'll wager he has the message now." He sighed. "The bad thing is I lost my fish."

CHAPTER FIVE

The Boy

Jonah left at once to go to the home of the minister to tell him about the death. A pink color was beginning to show in the east. "A new day is coming, Father," Jonah said aloud, and suddenly he felt his father's presence walking beside him. The white church with its great bell tower stood out in the dim light. Next door sat the small unpainted house where the minister lived. A light showed from one window. Jonah was glad he would not have to waken the man.

Reverend Gilbert had gray hair and a kind, tired face. "Your father's dead, is he?" he asked when he saw Jonah at his door.

"He is, sir."

The minister patted the boy's back as he held the door open for him to come inside. "It's a better place he's gone to," he said, and he sighed wearily. "Yes, a better place. Well, Patrick Hawkins was a good man. The church will pay for his box. I'll go to the casket maker right after meeting. We will bury him on the morrow, first thing." The minister also said he would send word to Mr. Samuel Hale. "Your father worked many a year for Mister Reynolds and then for Mister Hale; doubtless the gentleman will desire to be present to mark the end of his life."

Reverend Gilbert insisted Jonah have some hot porridge and warm bread with jam before leaving, and he sat with the boy as he ate. Chimes sounded from the next room. "That clock was in my home when I was a boy in London," said the minister. "It was almost the only thing we brought with us to this country."

"My father was a boy in London too," said Jonah. "He was a loyalist." He wanted to ask the minister if he too felt loyal to the king, but he thought perhaps he shouldn't.

"Your father worried for you, my boy. He felt your sister would likely marry soon, but he feared you would be without guidance." He removed his spectacles and rubbed his eyes. "These are hard times for men of all ages and will, I fear, get worse."

Something about the man's tone made Jonah feel more comfortable with him, and he decided to ask his question. "Are you a loyalist, sir?"

Reverend Gilbert leaned back in his chair. "I strive to hold myself above worldly concerns. I wish to be only on the side of peace." He shrugged and shook his head. "Such a path is not always easy to follow."

Jonah said nothing and busied himself with his bread. He knew about trying to take no side. When he had finished his porridge, Reverend Gilbert walked out of the cottage with him. "I will ring the bell now for your father," he said, and Jonah listened to the tolling as he walked.

At home, he found Mercy on her knees, scrubbing the kitchen floor. She looked up at him. "People will be coming in. I won't have them saying we live dirty."

For a time, Jonah sat beside his father's bed. He lifted up one heavy, lifeless hand, turned it palm up, and studied it. Years of work at sea and then in the mill, cutting the whalebones for corsets and collars and petticoat stays, had made the hand scarred and hard. Touching it, Jonah could feel the roughness, yet his memories of his father's hands were of the softness of his touch. Those hands had been, always to Jonah, gentle. When he put down the hand, he moved away from the bed.

He went, then, to the corner to lift up his father's small sea chest. It was something he would not leave behind when he left this cottage. The chest, their father's most treasured possession, had been always in the same corner of their home. It had a shiny black finish and a light oak trim. The boy loved the brass handles and the name on the front side, Patrick Hawkins spelled out in brass letters. "Cost me a pretty penny," his father had said. "Took my whole wage, it did, but I got it in my head to have it. I had me no family then, so I thought, why not?"

Jonah opened the chest. He took his mother's Bible from the table, where Mercy had left it after reading some verses to their father. Patrick Hawkins, able to write only his name, had never learned to read, but his wife had. She prized her Bible, and she prized education, seeing that both her children learned to read, and wanting Jonah to go on.

He looked up then to see Mercy. "Put the Bible in the chest. Wherever we go the Bible and the chest go with us. If the time ever comes, when you're a man I mean, and we go different ways, the chest is yours and the Bible mine." Jonah did as she said. He lifted the lid and thought he caught the smell of his father and of the sea. He knew he could touch it always and remember that his father's hands had been on that wood. Even when he himself grew old he could have his father with him.

Word spread quickly. Neighbors came after meeting, some bringing food. Their pine table had never been as full as it was that day. Jonah ate salted fish and little sweet cakes until he could eat no more.

The neighbors, he noticed, did not ask him or his sister where they would go. He also noticed that they kept their eyes down when they said good-bye. He knew they felt troubled because they could not offer shelter. The boy found no words to ease their discomfort, but neither did he feel resentment. His neighbors were poor. They could not take in orphans.

When the last visitor was gone, and the sun had set, the boy and his sister were alone with their dead father. "Should we sit with him?" Mercy asked.

Jonah felt surprised. Usually she did not ask his opinion. "What good would be served?"

She shrugged. "None, I suppose." They went each to their narrow beds. Sometime in the night, Jonah woke. Light from a bright moon poured into the cottage, and he saw his sister. She sat in the chair beside their father's bed.

I'll get up too, he thought, but he did not move, and his heavy eyes closed again immediately.

When he next woke, his sister was in bed. The light in the cottage now came from the newly risen sun. The undertaker, Jonah knew, would not bring his good coach, and, early in the gray morning, he heard the sound of the small cart, heard the wheels on the road and the bark of the little white dog that always followed. His sister heard too, and she rose to go to the door. Old Mr. James Richards, in black shoes, a black coat, and a black hat, seemed larger than his small stature. He came into their cottage with an air about him, the air of one in charge of death. The boy and his sister stood back in awe.

Just inside the kitchen he stopped. "Where are the remains?" he asked.

"We left him on his bed," said Mercy, and Jonah thought she sounded ashamed that they had not hauled their father into the kitchen so that Mr. Richards would have been less inconvenienced.

The undertaker followed Mercy and looked down at their father. "Quite thin," he said, but then he sighed. "Still, I'll need help." His eyes settled on the boy. "You'll do, I suppose. Come with me." Jonah trailed the slow black steps outside to the cart. They lifted the wooden box between them. With Mercy holding the door, they carried it inside to a place beside the bed.

Jonah helped the undertaker lift the body from the bed and lower it gently into the box. The box was heavier now, and they struggled. "Couldn't bring a helper," muttered the undertaker when they had gotten out the door. "Cost would be too dear, me not knowing if I am ever to be paid except for the box."

Jonah drew a deep breath. "I will pay the bill," he said. "Just write it out for me. We've things we can sell." His mind raced. The cow, of course. They couldn't take a cow with them to the poorhouse or an orphans' asylum. With a great burst of strength, he lifted his end of the box easily onto the cart and stood with his hand on the lid.

Mercy came to stand beside him. Mr. Richards climbed onto the driver's seat and urged his tired horse forward. With the white dog following them, the boy and his sister walked behind the cart down the lane. They passed the blacksmith shop. Just as they moved on to be in front of the tanner's, a cloud slid over the sun, and the boy shuddered on the gray path. The road turned upward, then toward the hill where the town buried its dead.

No rain fell, but the sky filled with clouds. Jonah worried that even a sprinkle would cause Mr. Richards to announce that he would not go on. Would he dump the box in the road and drive away?

He looked up then to see that Mr. Samuel Hale's coach waited on the hill. The undertaker would not be likely to leave his job unfinished, not with such an important man waiting. Just as the cart reached the summit, the sun broke through the clouds so that Patrick Hawkins, born in dreary London Town, was buried in New London on a sunny day.

A small group of neighbors had gathered. When the cart arrived, Mr. Hale stepped out of his coach. He came to help lift the box and lower it into the hole. "Father would have liked that, Mister Hale helping to lift him," Mercy whispered to Jonah when he came to stand beside her.

The minister took off his black hat and held it in his hand. In the other hand he held a small prayer book. "Our Lord said, 'In my father's house are many mansions.' Patrick Hawkins dwells in a mansion this day. May there be a place for all of this company there someday too." He looked at Jonah. "Take a shovel of dirt, boy," he said, and Jonah tossed the dirt onto his father's box. "Dust to dust," said the preacher. He prayed aloud then, asking God's guidance for them all, but especially for the two orphan children who stood now with no one to protect and guide them. When the prayer was done and the box was covered, the ceremony was over.

Goodwife Stevens, an older woman who lived just down the lane, came to take one of Mercy's hands in hers. "Mister Stevens and me, we've talked it over a good bit. We've but little," she said. "Still, we'll not see you turned out on the street. You can come to us and sleep on our floor if you've no better offer."

Jonah had not noticed that Mr. Hale had come to stand just behind him. Now the man moved closer. "It's generous you are, mistress," he said, and he took off his hat to bow to her. "I'll not force them, but I have hopes that Mercy and Jonah will come to live with my wife and me at Stone Croft."

Jonah saw his sister's eyes grow wide with surprise, and he felt her grip his arm tightly. Was this some strange dream? Mercy found words before he did. "Mister Hale," she said softly. "Oh, thank you, Mister Hale."

"We'll work hard," Jonah said. "We'll work as hard as ever you've seen."

Mr. Hale smiled. "That's what I like to see, hard work." He mussed Jonah's dark hair. "Your work will be mostly at school, though, and Mercy here, well, I'll leave her occupation to my fine wife. We've a boy of one year, and I am afraid he is a bit of a handful." He laughed. "Our little Tobias requires a good deal of tending for one so small."

"I'm awful fond of babies," said Mercy. "I'll make myself of use. You can be sure of that."

"When?" the boy asked. His voice sounded too high and nervous in his own ears, but he could not keep quiet. "When shall we come to you?" He should have waited for Mr. Hale to speak of when. He felt his face grow red.

"Now," said the man, and his smile made Jonah feel better. "There is no time like the present. Say good-bye to your neighbors, thank the minister, and we will be on our way."

They were about to climb into the coach when Mr. Richards came to press a small piece of paper into Jonah's hand. "My bill," he said. "The reverend says the church will pay for the box, but I've not seen any payment for anything as yet."

Mr. Hale took the paper from Jonah's hand. "You will have your money this afternoon, sir," he said.

Jonah felt relieved. He had been uncertain about how to go about selling the cow. Yet he felt slightly sorry too. He had liked thinking he could pay the money himself, had thought it something of a gift to his father.

Jonah had never ridden in a fine coach. They sat on bright red seats, trimmed with dark wood of a scrolled design. He looked out the window and felt somehow that he was looking at a different world. He turned his head, straining for a last glance at the newly turned earth of his father's grave.

"We can pack our things quick like," Mercy said when the carriage stopped in front of the cottage.

"There's our father's sea chest, you know, and we are much attached to it," said Jonah. "And we've a cow who will want milking. I'd like to take her down to the Stevens' place. It's just a space down the lane."

"Take your time to part with the place. We will wait for you," said Mr. Hale.

Jonah came back from delivering the cow to find Mercy inside, her arm resting on the sea chest that sat on the kitchen table. "I've put in your other shirt and pants along with my other dress," she said to him. "There is naught else, I think." She looked about, surveying the place.

The spring day had turned quite fine, but with no fire at the hearth a chill filled the cottage and went deep into Jonah's bones. "We were born here," Mercy whispered, and she reached out to touch the kitchen wall.

Jonah stood near the door, staring about him. He could still see his mother in this small house, going about her cooking and his father at the head of the table, Mercy on the bench, himself beside her. His throat was too full to speak.

"It was a good life we had," said Mercy. "Our mother and father did all they could to see we had what was needed."

Jonah swallowed and found his voice. "That they did." He moved away from the door and went to lift the chest. Mercy held the door for him. His feet grew suddenly heavy, and he marveled that he was able to lift them to move across the threshold.

The driver, whom Mr. Hale called Davis, jumped down to help Mercy step up and to take the chest from Jonah. The boy wanted to caution the man to be careful with the trunk. "It's a valuable piece," he wanted to say, but he held back the words. Davis would doubtless have been amused. Doubtless he was accustomed to handling truly fine pieces of luggage.

In the coach, Mr. Hale said but little, and Jonah was glad of no need for his own response. They drove through New London and took a road on the other side. After perhaps two miles, the coach turned onto a tree-lined drive.

"Oh," Mercy gasped, and Jonah stared out the window. A huge mansion built of gray rock stood before them.

"Welcome to Stone Croft," said Mr. Hale. "It was built by my wife's grandfather, the first whaler here. He had it constructed from stone taken from the very fields on which it stands."

"It's lovely," said Mercy.

The horses turned onto the circle drive before the mansion. Jonah struggled to take it all in. He had lived all his life in a two-room cottage. Suddenly, he wanted to jump from the coach, wanted to run. Would not the poorhouse be better? He could never be comfortable in this place, this palace.

The driver came to set up the step so that they could climb out easily. Jonah looked up to see his father's chest strapped on top of the coach. "Davis," called Mr. Hale, "will you hand down the chest?"

Jonah felt better when his arms were back on the chest. Just then coming out the door of the house and moving toward them was a beautiful woman, with her red hair piled in high curls on her head. The green of her eyes matched the green of her lovely gown.

"Welcome to your new home," she said. "You are to call me Miss Jayne, and"—she pointed with her head toward Mr. Hale—"Mister Samuel will do for my husband." She reached for Mercy's hand. "It will be jolly having another female here."

"Thank you . . . Miss Jayne," said Mercy softly. Jonah did not speak.

Stepping from the bright light made the house seem dark inside. At first Jonah did not see the servant who wore fancy pants and a bright jacket. "This is Phillip," said Miss Jayne, and the man bowed. "He will show you to your rooms. I've arranged for my tailor to come in this afternoon to measure you for new clothing." She reached out to touch them each briefly on the shoulder. "You may want to rest some before we eat. We are truly glad to have you with us."

Miss Jayne disappeared down the hall, leaving Mercy and Jonah with the servant. "Should I take your chest, sir?" he asked.

It took Jonah a moment to realize he was being spoken to. "Oh . . . no, thank you," he said when he had come to himself.

"Very well, then, follow me, please."

They were led down a short hall. "That's the nursery." Phillip leaned his head toward the first door. "The young man sleeps there as well as his nurse." He paused in front of the next door. "This is to be your room, miss." He opened the door. Mercy stepped inside. Jonah had a glimpse of a large bed with a flowered spread. He wanted to go inside with Mercy, but Phillip moved on. "This one is for you, sir." He opened the door and motioned for Jonah to enter. "I think you will find everything you need to be comfortable," Phillip said, and he was gone.

Jonah looked around. For a long time he stayed there by the door, his chest still in his arms. Finally, he carried the chest to a corner and lowered it carefully to the carpeted floor. He walked to the large bed in the center of the room and pushed down on the red-and-blue-striped cover.

Would he not suffocate in such a bed? He closed his eyes and tried hard to keep the tears from seeping out. Why had he been thrilled to be invited to this place? Come nighttime, he would take a blanket from the bed and find his rest on the floor.

He left the bed and moved to the hearth. No fire burned, but heat still came from the stone. Someone, doubtless a servant, had built a fire there in the cool morning. Why? Fires just for one person; he shook his head.

Against one wall was a small desk. Jonah pulled out the chair and sat down. His own desk! For the first time since entering the house, he felt a tingle of pleasure. There was a lamp on the desk, and it was full of whale oil! He could read, even after dark! Then he saw the pen, and his hand trembled as he reached to touch it. It was a fine pen made from a fancy white feather. Beside the pen sat an inkwell, and on the desk was a small stack of paper. Flipping the edge of the pages, Jonah marveled. Paper was expensive. There had never been a pen or paper in their cottage.

He picked up the pen, removed the cork from the inkwell, and dipped the pen inside. Did he dare write something? Would Mr. Samuel or Miss Jayne come tomorrow to check on how much paper was still in the stack? Mayhap that was part of Phillip's job.

He shook his head. No, if they had not intended him to use the paper, it would not have been left in his room. He took a piece from the stack and wrote, "In the year of our Lord One Thousand Seven Hundred and Seventy-Four."

He put the pen back in the holder then and sat staring at the words.

Suddenly, he remembered his sister. He could go to her room, couldn't he? After all, no one had said he should not stir. Still, he felt nervous, and he opened the door slowly, leaning out to look down the empty hall. He moved quickly to his sister's room. She was glad to see him. "Isn't it beautiful?" She pulled him in. "I've never seen a place so lovely."

Jonah looked around. It was a pretty room, much like his but with lace on the curtains and bedcover. "But, Mercy," he said, "I don't feel right here, don't belong. I'd rather be in our little house."

She led him over to a small settee, upholstered in a soft fabric with roses in its pattern. She sat down and pulled him beside her. "It's strange, I know, us burying our father this morning, and now all this." She waved her arm to take in the room. "I've been thinking, though, that he would be happy. Our father would be most happy could he see us amid all this finery."

"Mayhap he would, but, Mercy, I don't want to live here." With one hand he pulled at the sleeve of his roughly made shirt. "I've no wish to wear a rich man's fine clothes, either." He shook his head. "I'll tell the tailor just that when he comes to measure me."

"No!" It was Mercy who now grabbed his sleeve. "You will do no such thing, Jonah Hawkins! How would that look to Mister Samuel, you refusing to have new clothes? He can't have the likes of us going about practically in rags and living in his house." She choked back tears. "If you won't have the tailor measure you, we might as well get the sea chest and leave now."

Jonah got up and walked to the window. "Don't cry," he said. "I'll not refuse the new garments." He stared out at a lovely garden full of blue, white, and reddish purple flowers.

Crocus, the boy thought that was the name Master Hale had used when the same flowers bloomed in front of the school. "Be careful of the crocus," he had cautioned when the boys went out to games. A bluebird landed on a nearby tree branch. He felt tears stinging at his eyes again, but he willed them to stop. He would stay for now in this castle for the sake of his sister.

The tailor, a thin young man named George Stoner, took Jonah's measurements for new britches, shirts, and jackets. He brought his sister with him, and it was she who measured Mercy for dresses. "Does Miss Mercy have a beau?" George asked while he measured the length of Jonah's arm.

"No."

"How so?" He wrote down a number on the pad he carried with him. "I'd say that's a bit of surprise, comely girl such as her." He bent to measure Jonah's leg. "How old is she?"

"Sixteen."

"Of an age to be courted, I'd say." George Stoner smiled. "My sister is leaving my home soon to be married, and I think it is time I considered taking a wife. I need one who can help me with my work."

A rage came up from deep inside the boy. "My sister is not looking for a husband," he snorted. "And if she were, she wouldn't be interested in someone who only wants her to sew."

"You need not be so haughty," said George. "You've only just landed among the upper crust. Who can say how long you will be welcome in such grand digs?"

"Are you finished with me?" Jonah walked to the door and opened it. George gathered his pincushion, threw his measuring ribbon around his neck, and stalked out of the room. Jonah leaned against the door as if barring the man from returning.

At the evening meal, the boy was amazed at the food, so much of it. On the side table sat a big ham, a bowl of cooked pears, two loaves of hot bread, and a dish of sweet potatoes. He had not felt hungry since stuffing himself yesterday, but now his stomach felt suddenly empty. Before his father's illness, food in their cottage had been plain, but Jonah had not lived side by side with hunger. Of late that had changed greatly. What would it be like to live in a house where such a feast was served regularly? He wanted to eat. Why could he not be happier about living in this house where a boy could fill his stomach so easily each day?

It was too much. For a moment he thought of running, but Miss Jayne came from behind him to take his arm and draw him toward the table. "This will be your place, Jonah, across from Mercy." She moved on to sit at one end.

Mr. Samuel came then to take his chair at the other

end. "How pleased we are to have two new family members at our table," he said, and he smiled at Mercy and Jonah.

"Where's little Tobias?" asked Mercy. "Does he not eat?"

"Oh yes," said Miss Jayne. "He has but only started to feed himself, quite a mess too. He will have his dinner in the nursery until he is older and able to follow the rules of polite society."

Jonah dropped his eyes. What were the rules of polite society? He was certain he did not know, but he would watch Mr. Samuel. Doubtless he should not eat quickly, and he tried not to shovel food into his mouth. He tried to take small bites and swallow before lifting his utensil for more.

About halfway through the meal, Miss Jayne clapped her hands. "Oh dear, I forgot," she said. "I've heard the most amazing thing!" Miss Jayne leaned forward. "Samuel, your cousin Nathan plans to have classes for young ladies this summer! He's going to teach them from five thirty to seven thirty, before the boys come, and he isn't even charging their parents."

Samuel sighed deeply. "I know, my dear. Nathan got the approval of the proprietors before announcing it." He scowled. "I felt it shouldn't be allowed, but I was outvoted. Why should girls learn more than to read and write? They need to know only how to manage a household, don't you agree?"

She smiled slightly. "No, Samuel, I do not agree. In

fact, if ever we have a daughter, I want her educated alongside Tobias."

Mr. Samuel's face registered surprise. "My dear, I had no idea you felt this way!"

Her smile was big now and she shrugged. "You never asked." Then she turned to Mercy. "Would you like to attend these summer classes?"

Mercy swallowed hard, and her eyes told Jonah that she did not know what to say. He gave her a little nod, but she did not see. She looked at Miss Jayne. "I . . . would."

"Very well, then, you shall do just that. Perhaps we had best let Nathan know. He may have a limit on the number of young ladies he will accept, and I've no doubt a great many mothers will be eager for their daughters to attend."

"Really?" said Samuel. "May I ask why you think mothers will be so enthusiastic about Nathan's strange venture?"

"Because I do not believe women will see the idea as strange," she said, and laughed. "Besides, Master Nathan Hale is a fine-looking young man whose father owns a good deal of land. The mothers of New London will recognize the summer classes as a fine way to introduce their daughter to a possible husband."

Samuel looked at Mercy and Jonah, and he put up his hands in a gesture of helplessness. "You may as well know from the beginning," he said in mock sadness. "This is no proper household. I do not control my wife." Jonah saw the warm smiles that passed between Mr. Samuel and

Miss Jayne, and he liked the man more because of those smiles.

Miss Jayne took her spoon and tapped her glass. She turned her head toward the kitchen. "Missus Dally, our cake, please."

CHAPTER SIX

The Man

Things had changed in the life of Nathan Hale. He no longer tried to avoid Betsy Lawrence. When they sat beside each other at the evening meal and her arm brushed against his, he did not pull away at once. Rather, he would enjoy the sensation of warmth that rushed through his body. He would turn to Betsy and smile.

He liked Betsy Lawrence, liked her a lot. He had almost decided to speak to her uncle, asking permission to officially court her, when a letter came from his stepsister, Alice. "Nathan," she wrote. "My year of mourning is up, and I am afraid I will soon have suitors. One man on Sabbath last asked if I am ready to receive callers. I told him I was not yet ready. I do not wish to have your father select another man for me to marry, but I fear I may not be able to forestall him indefinitely. I am wondering, Nathan, what do you think I should do?"

He sat staring at the letter on the desk before him.

What should he do now? It was not honorable, this string-ing along two ladies. He had to make up his mind, had to decide whom to court. A knock on his door interrupted his thoughts. "Master Hale," Robert's voice called from the hallway, "Father wonders if you will come down to him in the parlor. He wants to talk to you. He sent me to ask."

Nathan folded the letter and slipped it into the desk drawer. "Tell him I will be right down." He felt uneasy. Why did Mr. Lawrence want to talk to him? As chairman of the school proprietors, the man was important to Nathan. Had he offended him somehow, or had there been a complaint about his teaching?

He made his way down to the parlor, but found it empty. Choosing a chair near a window, Nathan sat down to wait. A small table stood next to the chair, and Nathan drummed his fingers on the polished wood. When Mr. Lawrence came into the room, Nathan stood.

"Sit back down, Nathan, please. Make yourself com-fortable." Mr. Lawrence was a large man, and his head was almost completely bald. Beads of perspiration covered his face, and he wiped at them with his handkerchief. He closed the door behind him. "I'd rather this conversation not be overheard," he said, and then he sat down in a chair on the other side of the table.

Nathan waited. Mr. Lawrence fidgeted in his chair a bit before speaking. "I must say that I am not entirely comfort-able asking the questions I must ask you." He paused, but when Nathan said nothing he went on. "It is about Betsy. I must ask, what are your intentions toward the girl?"

Nathan swallowed hard, and he felt his face grow red. What should he say? He searched for words. "Sir, I . . . I like Betsy a great deal. I mean, what man wouldn't, sir? She is lovely and of fine character." He looked down at his hands for a moment. "Let me assure you that I have made no improper advances toward her. I would never do that, sir. You have my word."

"What I want to know is, do you plan to court her?"

Here it was, the question Nathan had dreaded. "I . . . I don't know how to answer that question."

Mr. Lawrence sighed impatiently. "Yes or no comes to my mind, young man. Try answering with one or the other."

Nathan rubbed at the back of his neck. "I'd like to, sir, court her I mean."

"Then your answer is yes?"

Now it was Nathan who had sweat on his forehead. "No, sir. I mean I can't say yes because there is someone else."

Mr. Lawrence frowned. "You have made promises to another young lady?"

"No, not promised. In fact, I have not spoken to the lady." Nathan made a helpless gesture with his hands. "I am afraid I am not worthy of either Betsy or the other lady. I can't seem to make up my mind which one of them I want to court. I know you will think me a Don Juan, but . . ." His voice dropped, and he did not finish the sentence.

"My niece favors you a great deal, young man. I'd say she rather expects you to declare your desire to walk out with her." Mr. Lawrence took off his spectacles and wiped at them with his handkerchief.

"So does the other lady."

"You are in a bit of a hard spot then, aren't you? Personally, I'd rather be chased by a swarm of angry bees than to have two women both expecting me to declare my love. Still, it is Betsy who must be my principal concern here. I am afraid I must insist that you tell her about the other lady."

"Yes, sir, you are right, of course. I'll tell her this very evening. I will."

Mr. Lawrence left the room then, but Nathan stayed, and he stared for a long time out the window.

All through the evening meal, Nathan could feel Mr. Lawrence's eyes on him, and he sat uncomfortably in his chair. While Betsy helped clear away the dishes, he went into the parlor, but he could not sit down.

When he asked her to go for a short walk with him, her eyes lit up like stars, and Nathan felt miserable over what he had to say. Better, he told himself, to get what had to be said over quickly. They had just gone down the front steps of the house, when he blurted out, "I am not worthy of your affection. There is another, a lady at home in Coventry—"

She interrupted him. "So you have spoken for her hand, have you?"

He dropped his eyes to the ground. "I haven't, but I have considered doing so."

She reached out to touch him quickly on the arm. "Is

she prettier than I am? You can tell me the truth. Do you care for her much more deeply than you care for me?"

He drew in his breath and tried to think what to say. This was not going as he had imagined. He knew not whether to be pleased or distressed. "She is not prettier than you. I daresay a lady could not be prettier than you are." He shook his head with misery. "I don't know which of you I care for more deeply. I will not ask you to wait for me. Doubtless there are many men who would all but die for the chance to be your suitor."

"I am not interested in many men, Nathan. I am interested in you. Oh, I will allow other gentlemen to call on me. My uncle intends that I do so, but I will tell you something that shall remain our secret. I do not expect to return any other man's affection, not as long as you remain unattached." She smiled at him and laid her hand on his arm. "Don't look so miserable. I shall tell my uncle I am no longer interested in you as husband material, but we shall see, Nathan Hale. We shall see. Now let us walk down to the river's edge and look at how the water reflects the moonlight."

CHAPTER SEVEN

The Boy

For two nights, the boy went to sleep on the floor, but during that second night he woke before the clock in his room struck twelve. He sat up on the cold, hard floor. "You're a pure fool, Jonah Hawkins," he told himself, and taking his pillow and blanket he climbed onto the bed and snuggled beneath the covers. He wore the new clothes delivered by George Stoner too, but he felt uneasy, as if he wore a disguise. After school, he often put on his old clothes and helped Davis in the stable, tossing hay for the horses or cleaning their stalls. He also liked spending time in the kitchen fetching water for Mrs. Dally or filling the wood box. He felt more at home with the servants than he did with Mr. Samuel or Miss Jayne.

Stone Croft sat on a hill overlooking the Sound, and often when the evening meal was done, Jonah would make his way down to sit near the water. He felt close to his father there and sometimes he would say, "I'm thankful,

Father, I am. It is wrong of me to be uneasy here. I'll do better. I will." He would listen then to the lapping sound of waves and try to catch his father's voice.

Mercy fit more easily into the new home than did the boy. Jonah tried to be glad, but occasionally when he saw his sister in her pretty dresses laughing with Miss Jayne or holding the hands of the red-haired baby Tobias while he practiced walking, Jonah felt resentful, as if he were losing her.

Only at school was he truly happy. He loved learning Latin and often repeated aloud to himself, "*amo, amas, amat.*" He loved the literature his teacher shared with him. He loved improving his penmanship, and he practiced that skill in his room at Stone Croft. Most of all he loved his teacher. Master Nathan Hale did keep his school, not with fear but by making his scholars wish to please him.

When there was time for games, Master Hale often played with his students. Jonah cheered with the others when the teacher kicked a ball over the building. He ran with the others to find the ball and laughed when they found it in the well bucket. And there were the barrels that sat still in front of the school. Those tall wooden kegs were items of much interest. Could the teacher truly jump from one to the other?

Best of all, though, was when Master Hale read aloud, usually for a short period after the noontide meal. For several days now, the piece had been *Cato* by a man named Joseph Addison. The teacher could change his voice for each character, and Jonah leaned forward on his bench, seeing it all in his mind. The noble Cato knew that Caesar was about to put an end to the freedom Roman citizens enjoyed. The body of his son, who had died in battle with Caesar's forces, had just been brought to him. Master Hale read the beginning of chapter five. Jonah could imagine Cato "sitting in a thoughtful posture, in his hand Plato's book on the immortality of the soul, a drawn sword on the table by him."

"Well," said Master Hale, "it is time we turn our attention to numbers." Jonah tried to hold back the groan, but the sound slipped out. The teacher smiled at the boy. "Cato will still be sitting with his sword when next we see him."

All that evening Jonah thought about the play. What would Cato do with that sword? He could not bear the thought that Master Hale might not read the next afternoon. Besides, he could not wait even that long. He would get to school tomorrow in time to read from *Cato* himself before lessons began. He felt certain his teacher would let him take the book to his seat for a while. He rose early, glad that the summer session for girls had not yet started. If it had, Mercy and other girls would be sitting in the schoolroom right now. Jonah would never have gone into a schoolroom full of girls.

Just as the sun came up, he pushed open the door. No one was about, and he made his way to the teacher's desk. There it was; the small volume lay on the edge of the desk. Master Hale was nowhere to be seen, but he wouldn't mind if Jonah read for a while, he was certain of that. It would not do, though, for him to be found standing behind the tall desk as if he belonged there. He would take the book to his own bench, but first he wanted to open the play and find act 5.

He turned the pages until the spot was found, but he couldn't take his eyes away from the words. Moving slowly and already reading the book that rested on the desk, he reached to pick it up. Suddenly his hand hit something, and he saw the crock of ink. The cork must have been loose because it tumbled out, followed by the dark liquid. Jonah saw the ink run onto the open page. He snatched up the crock. Not much had spilled, but a dark stain covered most of the page. He grabbed a handkerchief from his pocket and blotted at the page. The ink had soaked through, ruining two pages.

What should he do now? He waved the book in the air with the inked pages swaying back and forth until they dried. He looked at the door. The teacher would be coming in soon. He had been wrong to go to Master Hale's desk at all. He had no business touching his teacher's things without asking. He should have waited for permission. That was plain to him now.

He had to think what to do, but he needed to get away from the school so he could plan what to say to the teacher. Carefully, he put the ink where it had been. Should he close the book? No, then the ink might not be completely dry. He would leave the book open and leave his handkerchief under the ruined page.

He moved toward the door. Master Hale might be coming in at just that moment. He opened the door slowly and leaned out his head. No one was in sight. He decided to run, and he did, down the hill and over the little bridge that crossed the creek.

He ran without thinking about the direction. Finally he had to stop to breathe. He was, he realized, on the path to the cottage where he had lived with Mercy and his father. He left the lane and threw himself down on a big rock.

He could go to the cottage. If it was still empty, he might go inside and spend the day there, not returning to Stone Croft until time for school to be out. The next day he could tell Master Hale he had suffered from a sour stomach and been unable to attend school the day before. "No," he said aloud. He would not be able to lie to Master Hale.

Then an idea came to him. Mayhap, he should just wait a bit; wait until other boys came to climb the hill to school. He could go in with them then. Master Hale was sure to ask who had touched the book, but Jonah would not have to admit what he had done, not for a while. How much did such a book cost?

If he could but find some sort of employment, he could save his money. Then he could buy a new volume of *Cato* and put it on the master's desk. He might even admit then that it was he who had spoiled the other one. He pushed himself up from the rock and began to make his way back toward the school.

When he rounded the curve in the path, he saw Thomas Allen just ahead of him and called to him. Thomas turned to wait for him, and Jonah drew in a deep breath. He must, he told himself, act as if nothing had happened.

"I say I can get to the top of the hill before you," said Thomas when Jonah was beside him.

Jonah had no wish to race. His legs were still tired from his wild run away from the school, but he had often raced with Thomas. They were closely matched and each always eager to prove superior to the other. Jonah had no wish to do anything that would make Thomas question him or even look closely in his direction.

"Ah, Thomas," he said, "you know I beat you just the day before last."

"You won't beat me today. I'll wager half my corn cake that I touch the schoolhouse first."

"I'll not take your food from you," said Jonah. "I've meal enough in my haversack, but I will beat you."

"On the count of three, then," said Thomas, and they counted together, each leaning into a starting position.

"Three," they shouted together, and they threw themselves forward.

Jonah put all he had into the race and did better than he would have supposed, but Thomas reached out to slap the building seconds before he did.

Jonah fell against the wall, breathing hard. "I'll best you next time," he said, and Thomas laughed.

Just then Master Hale came around the corner. He held the bell in his hand. "Are you two just arriving?" he asked.

Jonah was glad when Thomas spoke up immediately. "Yes," he said, "and we raced up the hill. I won." His voice was jubilant.

"Inside with you, then," said the teacher. "You can put what's left of your strength into learning." He began to ring the bell.

The moment Jonah stepped inside, his eyes went to the desk. He could not see the book. He stood for a moment beside his place on the bench, his gaze searching. Could he think of some excuse to move closer to the desk? He hesitated. No, he had best sit down. He had to act as if nothing had happened. Still, he hunched quietly over his part of the table while boys chattered all around him.

When Master Hale entered the building all noise stopped. Would he mention the book right away? Jonah forced himself to look at the teacher. With relief he noticed that Master Hale smiled. Maybe he hadn't noticed the ink. Don't be foolish, he scolded himself. He had to have noticed the handkerchief. It was a certainty. Why had he left it? He should have closed the book and left things as he had found them.

"One of you has something you need to tell me," Master Hale said when he was at the front of the room. Boys looked from one to the other. Jonah made himself join the exchange of glances, his eyes questioned, but his heart pounded in his ears.

"Come now," said the teacher. "A lie of omission is yet but a lie." He looked from one side of the room to the other. Jonah cursed himself as he felt a heat grow in his face. Could others see that his face was red?

"What happened, sir?" asked little Timothy Green, and Jonah marveled at the small boy's courage. But, of course,

Timothy was innocent and unafraid. Jonah caught himself biting at this lower lip and quickly gave himself an inward shake.

"Should I tell you?" Master Hale spoke slowly, again searching the faces before him. "No, I think not. One of you knows of what I speak. One of you will come to me soon with the truth. I feel certain of that."

The room was totally silent. Then the teacher smiled. "But moving on now, I have news I think you will all be glad to hear. I could have told you yesterday, but I decided to save it until this morning. Yesterday the last Latin scholar conjugated all the required verbs, and for a while now all my beginning English students have been able to recite the primer rhymes for all twenty-six of the letters." A whisper rose in the room, and the teacher held up his hands. "Wait now, don't spoil the fun by breaking the no-talking rule." He waited, and the room became silent at once. "Today after the noon meal, I will jump from one barrel into the next, and . . ." He paused for effect. "I will even jump back into the original barrel."

The boys broke into a cheer. Jonah clapped with the rest of the school, but he felt miserable. He could find no true joy while guilt ate at him. He glanced up at the teacher who turned to look directly at him. Jonah smiled what he hoped was a natural smile, then dropped his gaze. He must find a way to earn money at once. Could he ask Mr. Samuel for advice? No, it would be too risky.

While Master Hale questioned the group about Shakespeare's plays, the boy's mind wandered, going back over the incident with the book. What should he have done? "Jonah?" The teacher's voice broke into his thoughts. "Jonah, did you hear me? Which play contains the words 'A horse! A horse! My kingdom for a horse!'?"

Jonah got to his feet. He knew the answer. He was certain he did, but nothing came to his mind. He looked down at the table. "I don't know, sir," he said, and his voice was full of misery.

"You don't know? That surprises me. We have read this play, Jonah. It's about a king." The teacher waited. Jonah could feel his eyes on him.

"I'm sorry, sir. I don't know," Jonah said again.

All around him hands were in the air. "You may take your seat, Jonah," said the teacher, and he called on another boy.

All morning time dragged for Jonah. Even history, his favorite subject, held no interest for him. Finally Master Hale closed the history book and moved away from his tall desk. "Before you go outside for your noontide meal, does anyone have anything he wants to tell me?"

No one spoke. "Very well," said the teacher.

Jonah stood to leave the building, but John Carver's voice broke into his thoughts. "Will you read *Cato* today, sir?" John asked. "I mean, even though there's the barrel entertainment?"

Anger shot through Jonah, and he pulled in his breath. Why did John have to bring up the book? He wanted to push his way around the boys in the aisle and move toward freedom outside, but everyone stopped and looked at Mr.

Hale. "Carry on with your noontide activities," said the teacher. "I will read from *Cato* at least for a short time."

Jonah breathed again and started to move. Then the teacher spoke again. "Jonah Hawkins, please remain inside for a moment."

"What crime have you committed?" Thomas whispered as he stepped around him, but Jonah did not answer. Instead he turned back to his place and sat down, his body slumped with misery. Even without looking up, he knew somehow that Master Hale did not move away from behind his tall desk.

The door finally closed on what must have been the last scholar because the room grew quiet. "Look up at me please, Jonah," said Master Hale.

The boy lifted his heavy head. Mr. Hale moved then, and neither of them spoke until the teacher stood in front of the table where Jonah sat. "Why did you lie to me?" he asked.

Jonah searched for an answer. Then words came to his mind. "I did not lie, sir. You never asked me if I spilled the ink."

Master Hale put his hands on Jonah's table, leaned toward the boy, and smiled slightly. "Well, not directly, but you knew about what I inquired. Lies of omission are still very much untruths."

Jonah knew he had to say something. "It was an accident. I know I should not have touched things on your desk." He put his face in his hands. "I am sorry, so awful sorry. I wish I had told you at once."

"I wish you had too." Master Hale reached out to touch Jonah's shoulder. "The truth is always best. Please make the truth your only way."

Jonah raised his head to look at the teacher. "What is my punishment?" he asked.

Master Hale did not speak quickly. For a long moment his eyes met the boy's. "What do you think should be your punishment?"

"I should pay for the book," he said softly. Then he spoke more loudly. "Yes, I should most assuredly pay for the book, but I do not know yet how I will raise the money."

"Actually, the book is not ruined, only one page." Master Hale laughed. "In truth, I have that page and most of the others memorized. I think I told you all about being in the play while I was at Yale."

The boy shook his head. "Even so, I should like to pay for the book."

"Let's make an agreement," said the teacher. "You pay for the book when you're able, and I will give you the stained copy."

"Yes, sir, I should like that very much, and I will be careful to tell the truth and not to lie by omission."

"Excellent! Now go and have your noontide meal." The teacher turned to go back to the front of the room, but just before the boy got to the door, he called out, "Jonah, let's make this episode our own little secret. No need to tell the others. Do you agree?"

"I do indeed, sir. I certainly do." Jonah bolted toward the door.

CHAPTER EIGHT

The Man

Nathan Hale was nervous. He knew he could jump from one barrel to the next, knew even that he could make the return jump. He had performed the feat many times. Waiting until his last scholar was down the hill, he had often gone outside and practiced. He knew he could make the jumps, but still his heart beat fast. Others might laugh at his wanting to make these boys proud of his athletic abilities. He was certain their former teacher would dismiss such a desire as prideful nonsense, but to him it was important. He controlled them by their desire to please him.

When he came out of the schoolhouse, all noise stopped. Nathan realized the boys must have practiced too, must have worked out in advance where they would stand, because without discussion they formed two lines on either side of the barrels.

"Very well," he said, "I see you are ready." They nodded, their faces solemn. This was, he knew, a big day for the boys.

For weeks he had heard their conversations. From time to time, one or another of them would express doubt, but for the most part they believed in their teacher's abilities.

Nathan carried with him a set of wooden steps he had constructed for climbing into the first barrel. He could have jumped, but he had settled on using the steps, saving the actual stunt. He placed the steps beside the barrel and climbed inside. From near the end of one line, he heard one of the younger boys say something, but the talk was quickly silenced by an older boy's "*Shh.*" He drew in a deep breath, gripped the top of the barrel sides with his hands, and he jumped, landing easily in the next barrel.

A great shout broke from the boys, but they grew quiet at once when he held up his arms. Then, with deliberate slowness, he placed his hands on the barrel and jumped again. The boys went wild. They clapped and beat one another on their backs. Then, to his surprise, they came to him, tipped the barrel, pulled him out, and, despite his protest, hoisted him to their shoulders. Carrying him above them they marched, cheering, back into the building.

The boys lowered him only when they were behind his desk. He stood laughing while his scholars made their way to their places. He held up his arms to quiet them. "That," he said, "was the best ride I've ever had!" Then he took up *Cato,* and he began to read. Even when he stopped reading and announced, "Back to lessons as usual," and the boys had settled down to work, the air of celebration lingered.

Nathan's mood changed drastically later. The last boy had gone home, and he was about to gather his things and leave too when visitors came. Mr. Lawrence and Mr. Matthew Green knocked at the schoolhouse door, and Nathan let them in. Nathan had only met Mr. Green briefly. He owned the *New London Chronicle* and was the father of little Timothy. A man in his early thirties, he was short and solidly built with dark eyes that held the look of a thinker. Both men were members of the school proprietors' board, and Nathan was sure they had come on school business. Had they come because they had heard about the barrels and thought such stunts were not suitable for a schoolmaster?

"Come in, gentlemen," he said, and he held the door for them to enter.

"We've come to discuss something, Nathan," Mr. Lawrence said when they were inside. They settled at tables near the back, where the larger boys sat. Nathan took a spot on a bench, his back to the table so that he could face the other men.

"First," said Mr. Green, "we want to say what a good job we think you are doing. My Timothy has learned much from you, and he came running home today with news of your incredible barrel jumps." He laughed. "He wanted to know if I could do the same. When I told him no, he was not surprised and expressed the idea that an ordinary man couldn't expect to be like Master Hale."

Nathan smiled. "I'm afraid my jumping talents are not greatly in demand in the world." He looked from one man to the other. "You didn't come to talk about barrels, though, did you?"

"No, we didn't." Mr. Lawrence sighed. "We came to talk about your cousin."

"Samuel?"

Mr. Lawrence leaned forward. "Yes, Samuel. You know he is a proprietor, one of several men on the board. We met this afternoon, or I should say six of us met this afternoon. We voted unanimously to ask Samuel to resign." Mr. Lawrence looked down.

"Samuel is, in many ways, a fine man," said Mr. Green, "but we don't want a Tory having a vote as to what goes on in our school. It's that simple."

"I see." Nathan's voice was low. "Have you told him yet?"

"No," said Mr. Lawrence. "A letter will be sent to notify him officially. We wanted you to know. The others felt we needed your assurance that you yourself do not have Tory leanings. I told them you did not."

Matthew Green nodded his head. "That he did," he said, "but we wanted to be sure. New London is largely solid in its support of the patriots."

Nathan stood and moved away to the window. He looked out at the hillside and said nothing.

"Well?" Mr. Green's voice was impatient. "Speak up, man."

Nathan turned from the window to face the men. "I am not a Tory, gentlemen. Yet I like it not that you felt it necessary to remove my cousin from the board. Is there no longer room for discussion and seeing both sides of the issues?"

"No," said Mr. Lawrence. "I am afraid such a time is gone."

A thought came to Nathan. "Jonah Hawkins," he said. "Samuel pays for his education, you know, and Jonah lives in his home." He left the window and moved back to stand in front of the men. "I am afraid he will take the boy out of school after this." He shrugged and shook his head. "I cannot say that I would fault him for doing so, but I would very much hate to see Jonah removed from classes." Nathan hoped that the men might change their minds, and he looked from one face to the other. "Is it possible you might reconsider?"

Mr. Green shook his head. "I am afraid our decision is made. I regret that Jonah will likely suffer because of it, but I fear Jonah's education will not be the only sacrifice laid on the altar of this unrest. Lives will be lost."

To Nathan's surprise, Jonah continued to come each day to school. Still, he wanted Samuel's assurance that the boy would not be taken out. He also wondered how his cousin had taken the proprietors' rejection. After a few days, he decided to visit Stone Croft. Phillip opened the door as usual, but Mercy Hawkins came to take his hat. "Oh, we are most pleased to have you here, Master Hale," she said, and her smile was wide.

Nathan thanked the girl. "Are you ready for our next class?" he asked.

"Oh yes, sir. I love coming to school."

"Good," he said. "I am glad I've had a chance to teach the girls of New London as well as the boys."

"Oh yes, sir," said Mercy. "I am glad too, ever so glad."

That didn't go so well, Nathan thought. He felt troubled

by Mercy's obvious and abundant affection for him. He did not want to encourage her, but he could not bring himself to be cold to her either. He did not want the girl to feel rejected or embarrassed. *I've got to think of some way to let the girl down easy.* Samuel came in just then and Mercy left the room. After the two men were settled alone in the library, Nathan expressed his unhappiness about the proprietors' decision.

"I know these men," said Samuel. "They think to pressure me into changing my mind. They believe I will crumble and give up my loyalty to King George." His lips pressed together hard, and he shook his head. "I won't do it, Nathan, not even if my beliefs should cost me much more than a place among the school proprietors."

"But you haven't kept Jonah away? I pray you won't."

Samuel laughed. "No, I will not punish Jonah because I am disappointed in my former friends. Besides, I have no fear that you will make a rebel of him. I have tried to instill my beliefs in the boy, but he tells me forthwith that he plans to join neither side, that he will remain neutral. By Jove, I believe he will do just that. He may be the only person in Connecticut who won't take one side or the other."

CHAPTER NINE

The Boy

It was that very evening, the evening of Master Hale's visit, that Jonah's life at Stone Croft began to change. Her name was Ebony. The boy read the name that had been newly painted on the front of the stall. "Where did she come from?" he asked Davis, and he put his hand over the gate to stroke the head of the beautiful new horse.

"Mister Hale brought her in today. Pretty little filly, ain't she?" Davis turned to look out the stable door. "Here he comes now."

Jonah looked up to see Mr. Samuel wave at him. "Did you see her?" he called. "She's yours."

Jonah whirled to look behind him. Was there someone else in the stable?

"I bought her for you, Jonah," said Mr. Samuel from the doorway. "It's time you learned to ride, and we're about to have a lesson."

While Mr. Samuel got his own horse, Davis showed

the boy how to put on the saddle and how to swing his body up and into it. Ebony seemed to know somehow that Jonah had never been on a horse. "She likes you," said Mr. Samuel when they had walked their horses out and down the lane. He explained how to use the reins. "Be gentle with her," he said, "but you must be firm too. She needs to trust you and know that it is you who is in charge."

They rode for an hour, side by side, most of the time slowly, but once when they had turned back to the stable Mr. Samuel urged his horse on a bit. "Let her go," he called to the boy. "Press your knees against her, and tell her to run." Suddenly, they were flying, not a horse and a boy, but a joined force, moving free. "Rein her in now," called Mr. Samuel, and Jonah did so reluctantly.

Every day he rode Ebony to school. Some of the others had horses too, and they tied them at the same post. None were as fine as Ebony, though. Some days during game time, Jonah would let other boys ride his horse. "You must never strike her," he would warn, "nor speak hard to her neither."

"She's the most beautiful thing in the world," little Timothy Green would frequently say.

Some days Jonah would let Timothy ride the horse to the newspaper office where his father put out the *New London Chronicle* and where the family lived in back. Smiling, Timothy sat tall in the saddle. "Like a prince," Jonah told him, "but you must go slowly, so I can walk beside."

Often on spring evenings, the boy and Mr. Samuel would ride together down the paths that wound through the fields and woods around Stone Croft. They talked little, but gradually Jonah changed. Once just at dusk, he urged Ebony to run. "I'll beat you home," he called to Mr. Samuel. The words had left his mouth without his preplanning them. He thought he should take them back, say he had not meant to use the word *home*, but the horse was running. There was no chance for a retraction.

"You won," called Mr. Samuel when they reached the stable.

"Yes," said Jonah. "I beat you home," and this time he used the word on purpose.

Life seemed good to the boy, but then the post rider came. Jonah learned about the news at school. Mr. Matthew Green had come to talk to Master Hale during game time. "We must help the people of Massachusetts," Jonah heard Mr. Green say, and the boy wanted to know more.

"You will hear talk," Master Hale said when the scholars were back inside. "I want to try to explain what has happened. Parliament, the lawmaking body over in England, has passed some new laws. They call them the Coercive Acts." He made his hand into a fist. "Many of us here in America call them the Intolerable Acts because we think their treatment of us cannot be tolerated. The Boston port has been closed. No food or goods of any kind can be shipped in or out of Boston unless the tea that was destroyed is paid for in full. The people of Boston depend on their harbor for jobs and for food. Also, the Massachusetts Colony will no longer be allowed to elect its own government officials."

Thomas Allen put up his hand. "Why doesn't Boston

just pay for the tea? It was stealing to throw it in the water, wasn't it?"

The teacher moved from behind his desk and walked closer to the students. "The tea did not belong to the men who tossed it into the ocean, and I do not approve of what they did. Still, I believe they were driven to strike back against unfair taxes." He sighed. "No, Thomas, no one will pay for the tea."

"Well, then, sir, what will happen? Will people in Boston starve?"

"No, the rest of us won't let that happen," said Master Hale. "In fact, I think this harsh treatment of Massachusetts will unite the other colonies. If rights are taken from one of us, they can be taken from us all."

"My father says he is ready to take up arms," said little Timothy Green. "Will you fight, sir?"

"I do not want to go to war, Timothy." Master Hale closed his eyes for a second. "I pray this dispute can be settled without bloodshed." He moved back to his desk. "I know I am breaking my own rule, talking too much about troubles outside our walls. Let us turn our thoughts to Latin."

After school, Jonah rode back to Stone Croft, and he thought about what Master Hale had said at school. Mister Samuel would not agree that the punishment Parliament had handed down was too harsh. Mister Samuel believed the men who had destroyed the tea were criminals. He was bound to be full of talk about punishment being given out where it was deserved.

As it turned out, Jonah did not see Mr. Samuel at Stone Croft. "He stormed out at noontide," Miss Jayne said when she came to his room. Her face twisted with concern. "He's all afire over the news brought by the post rider." She drew her eyebrows together. "There's to be a meeting at the tavern tonight to discuss what the men of New London will do. Samuel said he'd not be dining home this evening, rather going straight to the tavern from the mill." She clasped her hands together and began to squeeze one with the other. "I've fretted all afternoon. I am afraid Samuel will get into a row with some of the rebel leaders." She paused and reached out to touch the boy's arm. "Jonah . . ." She smiled, but her eyes were troubled. "I wonder if I might ask you to attend, to sort of stay back at the edge, not let Mister Samuel see you. I know he will insist that Davis stay outside with the horses."

"I am willing," he said. It was true he would be interested in hearing the talk, but still he felt uneasy. He shrugged. "But what is it you wish me to do?"

She put her hands to her cheeks. "Oh, I don't know, but at least someone would be there to call Davis if Mister Samuel gets into trouble with some hothead."

Jonah had his supper early in the kitchen that evening. Missus Dally, the cook, liked him and was glad to have him eating in her domain. "More lamb for ye?" She did not wait for an answer before piling more meat on his plate. "Grown right well ye have since you come to Stone Croft." She nodded with satisfaction. "That be a credit to my cooking, I'd say."

"Yes, ma'am," said Jonah before he filled his mouth again. He was nervous about the evening before him, but not too nervous to eat. It made him feel grown-up to be sent to the tavern. Miss Jayne wanted him to watch and listen. He could do that, and he could run for Davis if Mr. Samuel should need help. But Master Hale would be there. He would help his cousin. Surely he would, even though he leaned toward the rebel side. Family had to come before opinions. Family came before anything, didn't it?

Mercy came into the kitchen before he was finished eating. "I'm not easy with this," she said. "I wish Miss Jayne had not asked. You've no business being in a tavern with hotheaded men who'd as soon step on you as not. I'd rather you stayed quit of such a place. Tempers will be high this night. You're knowing that for a fact, are you not?"

He nodded. "I'll be careful."

"And Master Hale will be there, like as not." She smiled. Mercy had been going for two weeks now to the teacher's summer classes for young women, and she always smiled when she spoke of Nathan Hale. "Doubtless he'd let no harm come to you was he able to prevent it."

Missus Dally had gone out into the dining room, and Jonah wanted to say something before she returned. "Master Hale is a rebel, Mercy. Have you not heard him say as much?"

She shrugged and leaned on the cook table where he ate. "And what is that to me?"

Jonah fumed. Was his sister so besotted by Master

Hale that she could not see the writing on the wall? "It may well be a good deal to you, and to me." He reached out to grasp her arm. "We live in the house of a man who is a Tory, Mercy. Whose side will we take, our benefactor's or our teacher's?"

"I cannot imagine that anyone should care whose side we take, Jonah. We are nothing of import." She paused and cocked her head. "But should it come to such, I suppose we would take Mister Samuel's side. I mean we'd have to, wouldn't we?" She laughed. "That is, unless I was betrothed to Nathan Hale."

Jonah dropped her arm and jumped to his feet. "Mercy, has Master Hale given you any reason to think thus? Does he consider you in that way?"

She laughed again and shook her thick curls. "He has not, at least not yet, but a girl can dream, can she not?"

Just then Mrs. Dally came back with a stack of plates, and Jonah ran to the door to take them from her. "Thank you, Master Jonah," she said. "It's a fine gentleman you are."

He set the plates down, took his hat from the chair where he had placed it, and, with a wave to his sister and the cook, ran out the back door. The ride to the tavern was not long.

The trail ran beside the Thames River. The tree frogs were calling, and to the boy's ears their cry seemed a chant of trouble to come. He hoped Mercy was right, hoped no one would ever care what he and his sister thought about the trouble blowing across the ocean to America. He bit his lip. Well, at least, let it not be tonight. He wanted to go to the tavern to listen, but he had no wish to take a stand with either group. He might be the only person making his way toward that meeting who could see the truth on both sides.

Dark had just completely fallen when he reached the tavern. He could hear the noise coming from inside the building long before he got close enough to open the door. The hitching post was full of tied horses, and many others stood about, tethered to trees. He found a spot for Ebony.

There were carriages too, some with drivers on the seat. Jonah paused to locate Mr. Samuel's coach. He spotted it slightly away from the others and could see the dark form of Davis on the seat. Had Mr. Samuel called out to the driver to stop a distance away from others so they could leave quickly should trouble come?

Jonah slipped through the door. The light in the big room was dim, but the talk was not. Mr. Green, with a rolled copy of a newspaper in his hand, stood on a chair near the kitchen door. Men sat in other chairs, and many more stood around the room, all of them talking. Jonah strained to look at the faces around him. There was Mr. Samuel across the room, not far from a side door. He wore the white wig he donned on important occasions. His head was bent toward a shorter man with whom he was deep in conversation. Good! Jonah felt certain his entrance had been unnoticed. He pushed his way along a back wall. A portly man stepped in front of him, but Jonah did not mind. He could lean around the man when he wanted to see.

Spy!

"Hear ye, hear ye!" shouted Mr. Green, and he waved his paper. "This meeting is called to order."

"Who put you in charge?" Jonah could not see the speaker, but he knew from the tone that the man did not agree with Mr. Green's rebel views.

"I did," shouted the constable, "and this will be a peaceful exchange. No man will be shouted out from saying opinion, be he rebel or Tory." Clapping and cheers went up from around the room. Jonah noticed that Mr. Samuel moved toward the front.

"First to speak will be Mister Samuel Hale." Mr. Green stepped down.

Jonah leaned to peek at Mr. Samuel stepping up on the chair. The man held out his arms to the crowd. "I see many faces here that are well known to me. Some of you I do not recognize, but to all of you, friends and strangers, I want to say that I love my home. I love New London, and I love the colony of Connecticut." A cheer went up, and Mr. Samuel held up his arms for silence. "Let me go on." The cheering stopped. "I also love our mother country. I am a proud citizen of the British Empire, a proud subject of King George the third." Several men booed. The constable stepped up on a chair beside Mr. Samuel, and the booing stopped. "I have met the king." Jonah peeked out again and was able to see a smile on Mr. Samuel's face. "He is a kind man, a loving father to his fifteen children and to those he rules. A few short years ago, many of you fought the French alongside soldiers from England. Were we not all proud to be English then? What has changed?

Not our king. Most of you love the land on which you live.
So does our king. Do you know he is called Farmer
George because he so enjoys rural life? Parliament has
passed some laws you may not like. Yet is it not fair for us
to bear part of the cost for the war that drove the French
from America? Is it not fair to expect Boston to pay for
stolen tea? The mood of Parliament will change, but the
British Empire will not! Let us do nothing that will jeop-
ardize our place in the most powerful empire in the world.
I say, long live King George!" Mr. Samuel stepped down
amid cheers from a few men.

Mister Green took the chair again. "Next we will hear
from another man who bears the name of Hale. I give you
Nathan Hale, our schoolmaster and cousin to our last
speaker."

Master Hale stepped up, and Jonah could feel the ten-
sion in the room, almost as if the crowd held its breath.
They don't know him, the boy thought.

Seeing his teacher stand where Mr. Samuel had just
stood made Jonah know for the first time that the cousins
looked more alike than he had realized. They were different in coloring, Master Hale fair, whereas Mr. Samuel had
dark hair and skin. They were different in age, probably
by ten or fifteen years. But they stood alike both tall and
straight, both with the posture of a man who knew what
he thought and who was accustomed to being listened to
when he spoke. "I too am proud to be a British citizen,"
said Master Hale. "I am proud of the rights Englishmen
have enjoyed for many a year. Since the Middle Ages,

Englishmen have had no taxes levied against them unless their own elected officials voted to pay. Should Englishmen in America be treated worse than those living in England? I think not! I also think that Connecticut cannot stand by and see Massachusetts be punished for protesting those unfair taxes." It seemed to Jonah that everyone in the room cheered.

Other men spoke, more rebels than loyalists, but the meeting seemed peaceful enough. It was agreed to form a committee to gather goods to be smuggled into Boston. "No one will starve for doing what is right," said Mr. Green, "not if New London, Connecticut, can help it." Master Hale was chosen for the committee. Mister Samuel was not. When it became clear that the meeting was almost over, Jonah slipped out the door.

By the time men came out of the building, the boy was already on his horse. Waiting on the other side of the tavern, Jonah kept Ebony still until Mr. Samuel came out and climbed into the coach. "We'll give them a nice head start," he told the horse, and after a time he turned her toward Stone Croft. The ride was a pleasant one, a round full moon lighting their way. They had not traveled far when noise stopped him. Shouts reached his ears, men's voices. Jonah strained to hear the words, but he could not make them out. The sounds came around a curve in the road that lay just ahead.

Getting off the horse, he led her slowly. Almost at the bend in the road, he stopped. "Hale!" The name was clear. Someone had yelled, "Hale!"

Holding his breath, he moved forward just enough to be able to see. Two men had somehow stopped Mr. Samuel's coach. Both of them had cloths tied about their faces as masks and both muskets aimed at Mr. Samuel and Davis. "We've no hankering to hurt you," one of the men said to Davis. "You're just a working fellow like the rest of us." He thrust his gun at Mr. Samuel. "It's him we want."

"Take off your coat, Hale," said the other man. "Shirt too, and that fancy wig." He lifted a stick from a small wooden barrel that sat at his feet. By the light of the moon, Jonah could not make out anything on the stick, but he knew, knew even before he heard the terrible words. "We've got some tar for you, Mister Hale." The man laughed. "Got tar and a big bag of feathers."

A wave of sickness came over Jonah. He had once heard his father describe a man who had been tarred and feathered. "Big chunks of skin come off him, pulled the flesh from his bones. Fever set in then, and he didn't live long, poor devil. Paid a terrible price, he did, just for being sort of girl-like in his ways."

Mister Hale was about to pay that same price for being loyal to the king. "Move." He whispered the order to himself, and willed his legs to follow the command. Ever so carefully, he stepped backward, leading Ebony and hoping the sound of the horse's hooves on the road could not be heard. When he was far enough, he threw himself up into the saddle. Leaning forward, he urged Ebony to go. "Run," he told her. "Run faster than you've ever run before."

He would go back to the tavern, and he hoped Master

Hale would still be there or the constable. "Please, God, please," he prayed over and over.

Then he could see the lights, the wonderful lights of the tavern. In front of the building he jumped from his horse, stumbling over rocks in his path, but keeping himself from falling, he threw himself at the door. He did fall then, landing in a heap just across the threshold. "Help! You have to help Mister Samuel!" he yelled even before he sat up.

There were men around him at once, but he found Master Hale's face and kept his eyes fastened there. Someone offered a hand to help him up. He scrabbled to his feet. "They're going to tar and feather him, two men out on the road."

"Well," said someone, "it's no surprise, him talking like he does."

"It isn't right." Master Hale moved toward the door.

"I'm with you," said Matthew Green.

Jonah hurried to stay up with them as they mounted their horses. "I've got my militia musket." Matthew Green touched a wrapped object strapped to his saddle.

"Wish I did." Master Hale was on his horse, and Jonah urged Ebony forward.

"You ride down the road to confront them," yelled Matthew Green. "I'll stop a ways back and cover you from the path. Tell them you've friends with guns. I'll fire a warning shot."

They were moving then, and Jonah felt good that he could ride as fast as the two men. He glanced from time to time at the trees that seemed to be rushing past. "Hurry, hurry, hurry," he repeated to himself.

When they saw the carriage lanterns, he reined in his horse. "I fear they will have already hurt him," Jonah whispered.

Master Hale shook his head. "Mayhap not. They may still be only taunting him. Like as not, they'll scatter when they hear Green's gun. Their sort is usually a cowardly lot."

Slowly they approached the coach. Slightly in front of the horses, Samuel Hale stood naked on the side of the road. "Stay on your horse," Master Hale whispered to Jonah. "Ride away if you need to, fast." He was down then and moving toward the group. "Stop!" he yelled.

Jonah could see the men turn. One held a gun and one held a stick dripping with tar. He saw Mr. Samuel's back too, covered with that same black goop. Jonah wanted to get off the horse. He wanted to run to Mr. Samuel, wanted to wipe at the tar with his hands. But Master Hale had told him not to dismount. Nothing seemed real to the boy. Was he really on a horse surrounded by singing tree frogs while Mr. Samuel stood naked and wounded in the road?

"Stay out of this, school man." The man with the stick waved it in the air. "We just might give you some of what this Tory is getting."

"I know your voice," said Master Hale. "You can't hide behind a mask. You're Lyman Wolcott, and you must stop this at once." Master Hale moved to stand beside his cousin. "I have men in the trees, and they have muskets." Just then a gunshot sounded from beside the road.

"We wasn't going to hurt him much, just roust him about a bit," said the man with the gun. He jerked his head about, trying to see into the woods.

Jonah saw the one with the tar stick move toward the musket he had left leaning against the coach, but Master Hale saw the gun too, and he lunged. His hand reached the gun seconds before the other man. Quick as a streak of light, Master Hale twirled the gun, pointing the barrel straight at the man who had held the tar stick.

Another shot came from the trees. This one hit the top of the coach. "Shot high on purpose," Green shouted. "Right now I'm aiming square at a head. One of you is about to lose his. If you don't want to know which one gets shot first, I'd make for the horses now." Jonah saw then that Davis had untied the animals from the coach.

Grabbing the reins, they flung themselves into the saddles. "The constable will hear about this," Master Hale said.

"Let him hear. Little matter it is to us, who are on our way now to Boston, ready to fight," said Lyman Wolcott, and both men urged their horses to run.

Mr. Samuel had his pants back on now, and was full of gratitude for being saved. At least half his back was covered with tar, and without putting on his shirt, he climbed into the coach to be driven back into town to see the doctor. "Thank you," he said again from the open door. "Thank all of you."

"It was Jonah who saved you. He saw and came back for help," said Master Hale.

Jonah's throat felt too full to speak. "Ebony," he managed to get out. "It was Ebony, her being so fast."

"Matthew," said Mr. Samuel, "you were good to help."

"I'll not stand by and see a man tortured by bullies," said Mr. Green, "but I fear the day will come when the line between us will be drawn in blood."

"Surely we can avoid war," said Master Hale.

"If war comes," said Samuel Hale, "we will be on different sides, Nathan. I don't relish that thought at all, Cousin."

The coach was gone then, and shortly so were Master Hale and Matthew Green. Jonah was left to ride back to Stone Croft and explain to Miss Jayne what had happened. He wished he did not have to tell her. He wished he could get on a ship and sail to a South Sea island.

CHAPTER TEN

The Man

The teacher became a soldier, not an enlisted man, but rather a member of the New London, Connecticut, militia. He bought a musket, and drilled with it. He had hunted often back on his father's farm, had brought home wild turkeys, boar, or deer, but now he would carry a gun with thoughts of using that gun on a man.

At the Lawrences' home, he stood at attention, gun held upright, before the looking glass in his room. Nathan studied the image. After school the day before, he had drilled for the first time with the other men of the town. Hoisting the musket, he had followed commands. "Right shoulder, arms. Left shoulder, arms. Present arms." The men, twenty or so, were much practiced. The teacher worked hard to fall in with the group, which moved as if part of the same body. "We're ready," said their leader when the drilling was done. *Ready for what?* Nathan had wondered, but he had not asked.

Anna Myers

The commander, he knew, would have talked about how Redcoats, the king's soldiers, were all over Boston. Nathan did not believe those Redcoats would come to New London. Men of letters from every colony were writing long accounts to other governments around the world, explaining their grievances against England. Surely Parliament would grow more reasonable. Surely Parliament would take back the unfair laws, and the offended colonists could once more be proud Englishmen.

Just last week a note had come from his father. It was in the pocket of his waistcoat as he stood before the looking glass. "We are sending cattle," his father had written. "I'll not be an idle do-nothing whilst our brothers and sisters in Massachusetts go wanting." The letter had made him join the militia. He had written back to his father to say that he also would do his part. He now owned a musket, and after that first drill, he had been made a lieutenant, like Matthew Green.

"You're a scholar and a gentleman," said the captain who made the announcement. "We've a need for minds like yours to lead us. We must be ready if war comes."

Nathan felt compelled to accept the position, but he did not feel easy inside. His training was that of a teacher, a man of peace. He wanted to enrich young minds, not to scream orders to men in battle.

A knock sounded on the door. "It's a post for you, Master Hale. Father brought it from the rider." Nathan set his gun in the corner of his room to let Isaiah in. The boy looked down at the letter. "It's from Asher Wright," he said, "the friend you used to race with when you were younger, true?"

"Ah yes, you've a good memory. Asher and I were boys together. We raced, fished, hunted, swam, made a little mischief, but whatever we did, we were together." The teacher stood by the door, indicating that Isaiah should leave. There would be no stories tonight. A letter from Asher was a treat he wanted to savor.

His friend wrote of news from Coventry, the dance he had attended, a barn raising for a neighbor, the illness of a mutual friend. He also wrote about the work he did on the family farm. In the last paragraph, Asher turned his attention to advice. "Methinks your letter too full of Miss Lawrence. Doubtless she is charming, but are not many others equally as appealing? Only short weeks ago you wrote warmly of your stepsister. Be careful, old comrade. You are not yet ready, I think, to take a wife, not when your affections won't settle on one. Sitting beside the lady at meal each evening could indeed cloud your judgment."

Nathan smiled. This man knew him well. He had thought the mention of Betsy in his letter had been quite casual. Trust Asher to read between the lines, and, of course, he was right. Still, it troubled him when suitors came to the house to call on Betsy. The name *Don Juan* came to him again. Why couldn't he settle his mind on just one girl?

He folded the letter and put it with his father's. He would answer Asher soon, but now he had an appointment. Bonds had been formed that night on the road when bullies had been stopped. Nathan Hale and Matthew Green had become good friends, and the friends were scheduled to meet.

Downstairs, Betsy sat in the parlor with her knitting. "Good evening to you," he called.

"And to you, Nathan." Her smile was quick and sweet. He would need to think often of Asher's advice.

Outside he turned his steps toward the newspaper office that stood on a corner. He paused to bow to two women who were coming from a shop next door where ladies' hats were made and sold. In his office, Matthew Green sat at his worktable, but he jumped up when Nathan entered. "I've a bit of news for you," he said, and his eyes danced. "I want you to go with me to the Shaws' home. They have a houseguest named George Washington. I want to meet him, and I want you to come along."

"Why?" Nathan settled on a stool that stood beside the table. "I thought we were to go over a calendar to plan for militia drills. Who is this Washington?"

"He's a planter from Virginia, a man of some means. During the French War, he was an officer in the king's army." He pulled at Nathan's arm. "Come along. I've heard about this man. He's a leader of the movement."

Nathan did not move. "What movement?" he asked. "What are you talking about?" He did not smile, and he held out his hands in front of him. "No, I'm serious. What is our movement? I am inclined to want your definition."

Matthew let go of Nathan's arm. He looked down at

the floor for a moment before he spoke. "We move so that the people of these American colonies might be free of tyrannical rule."

Nathan did not leave his stool. "How far do we move?" he asked. "Do we move far enough to break all ties with England?"

"That, my friend, will be up to England, will it not? Was it not England that started this unpleasant business? Was it not England who taxed us without representation?"

"Actually, my friend, it was Parliament, a body of lawmakers, men who will be unseated in future elections or die in a long session and be replaced."

"And your point is?" Matthew raised his eyebrows.

Now Nathan stood. "My point is that I am an Englishman and proud to be so."

"Have you ever been to England, Nathan?" Nathan shook his head, and Matthew continued. "Aye, I thought not. Nor have I, and I say to you that I do not love England." He paused for a moment, shook his head, and continued. "I love Connecticut. I love the soft sweetness of a New London spring and even the hard wind that blows off our Sound in the winter. I love our Thames River, not the one in England. I love knowing that my Timothy will grow up here, and if I have my way he will grow up free of tyranny. I hope he will never be forced to bow down to a king."

"Your words are near treason. I pray you don't print such in your paper. I've no wish to see you hanged."

"Don't fret yourself on my account, Nathan. I know

the lay of the land. I'll hold my tongue and my pen, at least for the present. Now up with you. Let us make our way to the Shaw home and meet this George Washington from Virginia."

The Shaws, like Samuel Hale's father-in-law, had made their money through whaling. Their home was not far from the newspaper office, and the men walked. It sat proudly on a corner, well lighted in the spring night. It was a large house, comfortable looking, but not lavish. The teacher liked it very much.

"There he is," said Matthew Green, and he stopped during the climb of the front steps. "See there, sitting in front of the window. I'm all but certain that man is Washington."

"Maybe the Shaws have other guests," said the teacher.

"But look how he rests there, his demeanor. That man is important."

Nathan laughed. "Let's go in, Matt. There is no need to stand about outside and guess."

George Washington did, indeed, sit in a chair by the window, and he rose when Mrs. Shaw led the two guests into the room. He was taller than most men, even taller than Nathan, who stood a full six feet. His clothing was plain, but also plainly expensive. He wore no wig or powder in his reddish hair. His face was open and honest, his eyes, the eyes of a man who knew things.

Nathan Hale liked Mr. Washington at once. For a time, they sat in the Shaw parlor and discussed Parliament's attempts to punish Boston and all of Massachusetts. "I've half a mind," said Washington, "to raise an army of a thousand men, pay them myself, and march at their head to Boston."

Matthew Green jumped from his chair. "By all that I hold sacred, I am ready to march with you."

Washington laughed. "Note that I said 'half a mind.' There is, I must remind you, that other half. That other half says I must be at Mount Vernon for harvest."

Matthew's face turned red. "Forgive me my zest," he said, and he sat down.

"Not at all," said Washington, "but let me remind you of how important your work here in New London is. It is the newspaperman who can best fight for liberty. We need your words, perhaps more than we need your sword."

"Thank you," said Matthew Green.

Washington turned then to Nathan Hale. "And what of you, Master Hale? Are you too ready to join my nonexistent army?"

"No," said the teacher. "I am not ready to be shot at or to shoot at other men, for that matter. I am a schoolmaster and happy to stay in my schoolroom."

Washington looked long into the teacher's face. "I pray that you remain safely among your books and your scholars. Doubtless you teach well, but I am sorry to say, Master Hale, that I have a feeling about you. I think we will meet again. If we do, sir, I will ask then that you bear with me while I tell you a story from my time in the French and Indian War."

"Tell us now, Mister Washington," said the newspaperman. "It might be good fodder for my paper."

Nathan looked down to study the polished wood of the floors. He did not want to hear the story. Something about this man from Virginia made him slightly uncomfortable. He could not fathom why. He was about to say that he had to go, that he had another engagement, but Washington spoke first. "No, now is not the time for the story. Tell me about your New London militia."

On the walk home, both men were quiet for a long time. Then Matthew spoke. "Are you sorry I insisted you meet George Washington?"

"He's an interesting man," said the teacher.

"Well, he is willing to fight in defense of Boston. If I had to go to war, I believe I would like to go with Mister Washington."

"I do not want to go to war with Mister Washington or anyone else," said Nathan.

"But," said his friend, "if it comes to war, you will fight, won't you? I mean, you have joined the militia."

"I would fight if Connecticut were attacked," he said. "Beyond that I cannot say for a certainty." He laughed. "Of course, I know I will never die in battle."

"Now there's a story I'd be pleased to hear," said his friend. "Why do you have such faith?"

"Obviously, I've never told you about my neck."

"Your neck?"

"Yes, I have a mark on my neck, just in front." He pointed. "Hidden by my shirt. It's a big round mole, all brown and hairy. When I was younger, a group of us used to swim on hot days in the big pond over by the cemetery.

The boys would taunt me by saying I bear the mark of the noose. They would joke and shout out that I would hang one day."

"Surely you don't believe such nonsense?"

Nathan laughed. "No, but mayhap the notion has kept me honest. No robbing or plundering for me."

CHAPTER ELEVEN

The Boy

All that summer the boy worried. He worried about his sister and about Miss Jayne and baby Tobias. He worried most about Mr. Samuel.

Mercy was becoming more and more besotted by the teacher. "Master Hale says this or that" was part of her conversation at each evening's meal. "He read part of the most wonderful play, called *Cato*. You can't imagine how sweet his voice is," she said on a day when the Hales had gone out for the evening.

Jonah could stand no more. He looked up from his plate of lamb and carrots. "Mercy," he said, trying not to let his voice be hard, "can you not hear how foolish you sound? Has Master Hale ever given you one sign of encouragement?" He put down his cup with a bang.

"Why, of course he has." Her expression was shocked. "He encourages us all, says that a girl can have as fine a mind as a man's, and one morning he said to me that my elocution was superior."

Jonah spoke slowly, choosing his words carefully. "I do not refer to your education, as I think you know. You all but swoon when you speak of the man. I mean has he ever given you encouragement to think of him in a romantic way?"

Mercy was not finished with her meal, but she stood anyway and folded her arms. "Jonah Hawkins, you leave me be. Soon enough I'll be forced to settle for a husband from among the likes of Stoner the tailor, but for a time, leave me have my dreams." She hurried out of the room.

Jonah finished his meal alone. Well, as long as Mercy knew her hopes were without foundation, he supposed he could stop his fretting on her behalf. That left only his benefactor and his wife to worry over. Since the night of the tar and feathers, he had become more alert when he happened to be in public with Mr. Samuel. Often he noticed that a shopkeeper would scowl at Mr. Samuel's back, or he would hear the word *Tory* whispered with disgust. The boy did not understand why people had to despise those who disagreed with them.

At school, Master Hale still insisted that each person had a right to think for himself, and he would allow no name calling or jeering because one boy thought differently from another. Once, the boy found a chance to question the teacher about honoring opinions. Jonah had lingered at his desk, waiting for the other boys to leave at the end of the day. He had something he wanted to ask in private. Little Timothy Green took forever to gather his things, and Jonah folded his arms, waiting.

Finally, when Timothy was gone, Jonah was ready. "You do not agree with Mister Samuel's loyalty to the king, yet you still consider him a kinsman," he said.

Master Hale looked up from his tall desk, where he had been writing with his pen. "That is so, Jonah. You know I believe each man is free to decide for himself about matters of government." He went back to his work.

Jonah stood and moved to the front of the room. "Yet," he said, "if war were to come, your cousin and you would be on different sides. Could you, say, shoot at him in battle or run him through with a bayonet?"

The teacher smiled. "There you have it. Such is the reason we must avoid war. We cannot have kinsmen or neighbors fighting on different sides. This disagreement with England is but a family squabble. It must be settled without bloodshed."

Jonah was not satisfied. He moved to stand directly in front of the desk. "But if war did come, and if you found yourself in a battle with Mister Samuel, would you shoot at him?"

Master Hale did not answer at once. He turned and stared out a nearby window. Then he spoke slowly. "If ever I believed strongly enough in a cause to go into battle, if ever I became a real soldier, not just a home guard then, yes, I would shoot at any man on the other side. It is what soldiers do, Jonah. Their cause must come first."

"I wish all this business had never started," said Jonah. "Such wishes abound in every colony."

That very evening, an incident caused much concern at Stone Croft. They sat in the dining room for the evening meal. Miss Jayne had just called to Mrs. Dally to bring in the pudding. The sound of shattering glass broke into the room.

Jonah jumped from his chair, as did the others. Glass covered a part of the shiny dining-room floor and scattered over the food still standing on the sideboard. Amid the glass on the floor lay a large stone, a piece of paper tied about it with string.

Mister Samuel ran to look out the window. "The coward is not in sight, as to be expected." Jonah had run to get the rock. He picked it up and held it out to Mr. Samuel, who had turned away from the window.

"Does it say anything?" cried Miss Jayne.

Her husband took off the twine first, then read, "Get out, Tory." With the note in his hand, he moved toward the front hallway. "I'm going out to have a look-see about the grounds."

Jonah jumped up from the floor. "I'll go with you," he said.

"No." Miss Jayne ran to grab her husband's arm. "You mustn't! They could be out there still. They could pick you off with their muskets!"

Mister Samuel pulled from her grasp. "So what am I to do, Jayne? Cower in Stone Croft the rest of my days?" He moved away with Jonah right behind.

Outside, they walked around the house, searched the stables, and knocked at the door of Davis's small room.

When the driver came to answer, Mr. Samuel told him what had happened. "Cursed scoundrels!" Davis made a face. He reached behind the door and brought out a musket. "I'll look about in the trees."

"Thank you, Davis," said Mr. Samuel. "I'd best go inside and soothe Miss Jayne. She's beside herself."

Without announcing his attention to do so, Jonah followed the driver. They exchanged no words until they had tromped through the woods near the house. Back in front of the stables, Davis stopped and searched the grounds with his gaze. "Can't say I hold with Mister Hale's opinions, but I'll not see this family hurt. That I won't!"

Jonah said nothing, but inside himself he made the same declaration. He would do anything to protect the Hale family. He walked slowly toward the door of Stone Croft.

The winter came, and the boy carried firewood to school each day as did the other scholars. The fire in the little red schoolhouse burned bright as snow fell around it. On the town square, the fire was bright at the newspaper office, as bright as was the fire in the heart of the editor, who waited each evening after school for his friend the teacher to stop by his office to discuss the state of affairs between England and her colonies.

All winter the boy worried about his benefactor. Now he saw a more open display of loathing for the occupants

of Stone Croft. Those who worked for Mr. Samuel continued to be polite, but when Miss Jayne invited her friends,
ladies from the more prominent families, to a holiday tea
just before Christmas, only two of them came. "Oh my,"
said Miss Jayne to her guests, "it would seem the others
have forgotten the date." She forced a high, mirthless
laugh, then said, "Very well, all the more food for us."
Without waiting for the serving girl, she began to pile
sandwiches onto the china tea plates.

George Stoner, the tailor, had never come to ask Mr.
Samuel's permission to call on Mercy, and she was relieved.
"I've no desire to spend my life doing tailor work for my
husband," she told Jonah when he teased her about the
suitor. They would both laugh, but the boy could not smile
when George bluntly told him why he was no longer interested in Mercy.

He had come to take measurements for new curtains to
cover the parlor windows. "I need your assistance, please,"
he said to Jonah, who walked through the room. "My sister has gone off with her new husband and left me without
help. Write down the numbers I call out to you, and mind
that you are neat." He held out the pad and pen, then spun
back to the window.

Jonah wanted to throw the pad at the man, but he said
only, "Yes, I can write plainly."

"Six yards," called George. He measured again. "Four
yards. Did you get that?"

"Yes," said Jonah.

"Six again." George Stoner stopped to peer out the big window. "There is your sister. A buxom flower, but alas, this is a Tory household. I don't want my name associated with it." Jonah threw down the paper and pen, and without a word he walked from the room.

CHAPTER TWELVE

The Man

Elected men from all thirteen colonies traveled to Philadelphia, Pennsylvania, for a gathering called the Continental Congress. Word from that meeting came to New London by way of a post rider. Matthew Green took the dispatch from the hands of the weary horseman and went straight to work on his newspaper.

"Listen to this quote." Green still stood beside his press, but he motioned his friend toward a chair. "It's from a fellow named Patrick Henry, hails from Virginia." He took up a paper and began to read. "'Our chains are forged! Their clanking may be heard on the plains of Boston! I know not what course others may take, but as for me, give me liberty or give me death!'"

"Those sound like words of war," said Nathan. "So the Congress is saying we should fight?"

Green shook his head. "No, wait now. Let me finish the story. The Congress sent an appeal for peace to the king, but they declared there would be no English imports or exports, no trade at all until Parliament repeals the unfair laws."

Nathan leaned back in his chair. "It seems not all the delegates are as eager for war as Mister Patrick Henry is. Do you plan to print the hothead's words?"

"Yes," said Matthew Green. "I will print his words, and I will tell you something, Nathan. I agree with him. By all I hold holy, I agree!"

"Well, I still think Parliament will see their error." He got up and began to move about the shop. "Surely there are enough reasonable men in that body to recognize what needs to be done."

"I hope so," said Matthew. "I know you think me a warmonger, but I am not. I have no wish to shed blood or to bleed. However, I do believe there is no other path for America. We must break with England. 'Give me liberty or give me death.'"

Just as spring was changing the New London countryside, news came from Massachusetts. The post rider had ridden all day and night to bring the word. He went first to the newspaper office. Matthew Green listened to his news, and reluctantly took time to give the rider a meal and a bed before rushing out to spread the word. He went first to the schoolhouse.

"It has started," he told Nathan Hale, who had stepped outside to talk. "A rider came in this noon. I've given him a cot at the print shop. He is there sleeping, but he wants to talk at the meeting." He reached out and grabbed his friend's arm. "The man was in both battles, fought the Redcoats himself." He drew in a deep breath. "I'll tell you, Nathan, it makes your blood run cold to hear him tell of it."

"What happened?"

"Two battles were fought yesterday." He began to speak quickly. "The Redcoats set out to Concord to destroy the supplies the militia had stored there. At Lexington some seventy or so militiamen tried to hold the Redcoats back, but the Massachusetts men took a beating. Word spread, though, and by the time the king's men got to Concord, the colonists outnumbered them. The patriots pounded them a good one at Concord's North Bridge. Likely three times more British fell than Americans, and the Redcoats were chased as they hightailed their way back to Boston."

"So the fighting has begun," said Nathan.

"It has. We will show the bloody king what Americans can do." Matthew moved down the schoolhouse steps. "Meeting at six in the tavern; spread the word to any man you meet."

Nathan leaned heavily against the outside wall. Finally, he drew in a deep breath and returned to the schoolroom, but he made no effort to teach. "Holiday," he announced. "I am sorry to tell you that battles have been fought in Massachusetts between the militia and the king's soldiers." He looked down. "I'll tell you true. I have need to let you go. I must spend this day in prayer. I've decisions to make. But come what may, I'll be here tomorrow."

When the scholars were gone and the building was

quiet, Nathan Hale knelt for some time beside his desk. Then he took his hat and jacket from the hook and went out to walk. He walked up hills and stood looking down at farmland that had been plowed for spring planting. He walked through woods and leaned for a while against the trunk of a white oak tree to listen to the song of a bird. He vaulted over stone fences to walk through pastures where cattle grazed, and he moved down the path beside the river. In a small slough, he watched a pair of loons. One swam with two babies on its back. By the time he made his way toward the town, his decision was made.

At the tavern, the crowd was large well before the appointed hour of six. When Nathan came in, he saw that the tables were already full. Men stood about in groups talking excitedly. His cousin was not in the group. None of the other men who had voiced loyalty to England at the last meeting were present either.

Matthew Green turned from the group with whom he spoke and put his arm around the teacher's shoulder. "Nathan," he said. "I looked for you this afternoon, but you were nowhere to be found."

"I went walking."

"And what did you see?" asked Matthew.

"I saw Connecticut."

"Good," said Matthew. "I am glad you saw Connecticut." He moved then toward the front of the room and the chair upon which he would stand.

"Hear ye, hear ye," he called from the chair. "This meeting has commenced. Some of you will, undoubtedly, want to speak, but first let us listen to a man who was there, a man who fought both battles only yesterday and who has ridden all the way to tell us the news."

"My name is Aaron Rivers, and I hail from Lexington. We were warned by Paul Revere, warned that the king's regulars were coming our way. They wanted to capture Samuel Adams and John Hancock and hang them for treason. Besides which, they planned to destroy all the arms stored away by the militia in Concord. Ready we was when the Redcoats came, but our resolve was weak. Nary a one of us was unafraid, staring at them British soldiers all dressed up in fine uniforms and practiced like they was. Yes, I admit we was too scared. We was told not to fire unless we got fired upon, and our legs was weak.

" 'Disperse, ye rebels, disperse in the name of the king,' their major yells out at us. You got to see the way of it, with about seventy of us and several hundred of them and their fine guns, us with mostly our old muskets, used for hunting."

He paused for a breath, and someone from the crowd yelled, "Go on."

Aaron Rivers held up his hand. "I will, brother," he called. "Didn't I ride all this way to tell my story?" He nodded his head vigorously as if to answer his own question. "Our captain, he tells us to go home, but to stay ready. Some of us, though, don't start to walk away. Somebody fires a shot. Who? I can't rightly say whether 'twas us or them, but the Redcoats all start shooting. Eight of our men lose their lives. One man falls just outside his own door . . ." He paused a moment, and when he started again his voice was not so full. "We gather us up again, and we head for Concord to join up with that town's militia. Well, let me tell you like it was. The men in Concord was as scared as ever the men in Lexington. None of us fired whilst the Redcoats they went about like as they owned the place, taking guns and ammunition. Then smoke starts to rise up in the sky, and we know the brutes are burning the town, us just watching. That smoke, it plumb takes the fear from us, and our commander, he yells 'Fire!' We do, right there at that bridge, we commence to killing Redcoats. They're startled on account of they never thought we'd have the guts to shoot. They start to run, and, brothers, we start to chase them. I tell you it done my heart good to see their backs thataway. And we had us a man on fife and one on the drum. They played that song, you know, 'Yankee Doodle.' They made it up to poke fun at us, but we played it whilst they run. It's our song now!" He clapped his hands with joy. "I come to call you to arms, but I tell you true, it is no small thing to fight!" He stopped talking suddenly and turned back to Matthew Green.

"Thank you, friend," Matthew shouted, and he started to clap. "Thank you for fighting and for riding to spread the word to Connecticut." Aaron Rivers hopped down from the chair.

"We've got to fight too," yelled someone from the crowd. "There's no holding back now. Blood has been spilled." Others began to call out comments.

The newspaperman held up his hand. "One at a time, let him who wants to speak, come to take the floor."

"I'll speak," called a man who climbed upon the chair that stood beside Matthew's. "I am not saying I won't fight," he said, and he wiped at his forehead with his handkerchief. "No, I ain't saying I won't fight, but still and all, it's no easy thing to leave our fields just at planting time. Maybe it is that we ought to wait, see what it is that happens." He stepped down.

"No!" shouted another who climbed up. "If we go now, mayhap we will be back by a late planting time. All that's to be done is to show the king we mean business and do not intend to be treated like slaves."

Nathan Hale shook his head. Once their guns were picked up the die would be cast, and he felt certain the soldiers would not be back in time to plant this year. He looked down where the mud from the Connecticut countryside still marked his boots. He had not come to this meeting with any plan to speak, but he felt himself moving to the front.

"Ah," said Matthew Green, "I see my friend the schoolmaster has something to say." He made a sweeping gesture with his arm. "I give you Nathan Hale."

Nathan drew in a deep breath. "Let us march," he said. "Let us march at once." A great cheer broke from the crowd.

Only one more person spoke. Reverend Gilbert climbed up to speak. "For a long time, I claimed to be above all this, but doubtless it is time I took a stand. I want you to take the church bell, melt it for cannonballs. When next that bell sounds, it will sound for liberty." The crowd cheered and clapped. The minister held up his hand. "Let me say one more thing to those of you who go to fight. The Lord bless you and keep you."

Men stood about talking and planning, but Nathan made his way through the group toward the door. He would go back to his room and write letters to the proprietors of New London school. It would be necessary for him to obtain their permission to leave the school early. He would need to be excused from his contract if he were to march to Massachusetts to fight.

At the Lawrence house, however, he did not go inside. Instead, he walked to the stable. Another thing needed to be done, and he saddled his horse. Before he wrote those letters, he needed to make a visit. He needed to see his cousin.

At Stone Croft, he was surprised to see lights in many parts of the house. He had thought he might not be able to go in at this hour. He knocked at the door, but it was not opened at once. Instead a voice called out, "Who goes there?"

"It's Nathan Hale," said the teacher. "I've come to speak with my cousin." He heard a bolt slide, and the door opened slowly. "You're to come in," said Phillip, the butler. "Mister Hale will see you. He's in the dining room."

Samuel wore no waistcoat, his shirtsleeves rolled above his elbows. He stood beside an open wooden chest, and Nathan noticed that the china cabinet beside him was half empty. "We're packing," said Samuel. He looked into the teacher's eyes. "We can't take everything, but Jayne wants these dishes."

"Where will you go?"

"To New York. We leave tomorrow after I've put my business affairs in order." Samuel ran his hands across his face. "My holdings here must be dissolved, the mill closed down until it is sold." He turned back to the cabinet to remove some plates. "Do you know the Allens from the other side of town?"

The teacher nodded. "The boy, Thomas, is one of my students."

"Just so," said Samuel. "Their house burned this evening. It was no accident, Nathan."

"Oh no! Did the family escape?"

"Only barely. They are left with almost nothing and have gone to New York. They sent a servant to tell us." He closed his eyes. "How did it come to this, Nathan? I cannot for the life of me grasp exactly how it all came to be. I never would have believed when I came to this fine home as a bridegroom that I would flee it one day in fear for my life and the lives of those who depend on me."

"I wish it could be otherwise," said the teacher. "I've come to tell you that I am applying to the proprietors for an early leave of the school. Men from New London will march tomorrow to Massachusetts, and I will join them as soon as I am given leave from my teaching post."

"So our paths have come to a split in the road." Samuel Hale put out his hand. When the teacher took it, Samuel used his other arm to draw his cousin to him. "I wonder will we ever see each other again." He released the younger man and stepped back to look at him.

"Of course we will," said the teacher. "This disruption can't last forever."

"I pray you are correct. Would that we may dine together again here in Stone Croft." He looked about him. "We leave almost everything here. Davis and Mrs. Dally will look after the place. Mayhap when word spreads that I am gone, those who feel compelled to strike at all who are loyal will leave the house be."

"May I say good-bye to Jonah?"

"He's asleep, as is Mercy. They were already abed when the Allens' man came. We have not told them yet that tomorrow we will leave, having reached the decision just of late." He shrugged. "I don't know that they will choose to go with us, but it is my hope. Jayne and I have grown quite fond of them both."

"And they of you, rightly so." Nathan Hale turned toward the door. "Well, then, it's away with me. Doubtless you've much to do."

"I'll send the boy to you tomorrow before we leave. Certainly, he will want to say good-bye."

Outside the house, Nathan turned to look back once. In an upstairs window, framed by the light, stood Mercy Hawkins. Evidently Samuel had been wrong about Mercy sleeping and about her not knowing of the move because she lifted the sash. "Master Hale," she called, "good-bye to you, sir, and blessings on you."

Spy!

Nathan waved to her. "Godspeed on your journey," he called. *At least*, he thought, *I'll no longer have to worry about Mercy's affection for me.* It was not enough to make him feel really better, and he rode back to his lodging with a heavy heart. The storm that had so long threatened had come crashing into Connecticut.

All the next day at school, Nathan expected Jonah. While the younger scholars recited their lessons, he kept his eyes on the back door, waiting. During game time, he kicked high and thought the boy would be climbing the hill when the ball rolled down it.

Finally, just before dismissal time, Nathan looked up to see the boy had come soundlessly in the door and lingered near it, his eyes cast down. He left his desk and moved to meet him. He put his arm around the boy and drew him to step just across the threshold, leaving the door open.

"So you've come to say good-bye," he said.

Jonah looked up then, his eyes blinking back tears. He pointed with his head toward the schoolroom. "Most hate me now because the fighting has started." He bit at his lip. "I don't even know if I am a Tory, but I'm leaving the only spot I've ever known because of it."

"You've little choice, Jonah, not after what Samuel has done for you. Besides, there's your sister to think of and no place here for you to live."

"Could I not live with you, sir? I could work for you. I've no desire to go to New York."

Nathan put his hand on the boy's shoulder. "I'll be leaving soon myself. I plan to join the army."

"So you will fight with the rebels?"

"I like to think we may call ourselves patriots rather than rebels. We will fight until Parliament changes its unfair laws and withdraws the king's regulars from America."

Jonah pointed then to the black horse, tied at the hitching post in front of the building. "There's the horse." His voice shook slightly, but he did not cry. Instead he swallowed hard and went on. "I can't take her with us, and I thought about Timothy. You know, Timothy Green, I thought he might like to keep her for me. I mean, I know he's fond of her, and she will want riding. Would you ask him for me, sir?"

"I will," said the teacher.

The boy backed away. "And could you take her back to Davis at Stone Croft if Timothy can't keep her?"

"I'll see to the horse, Jonah."

"Good-bye, sir." Jonah turned then and ran down the hill where his sister and the Hales waited. The teacher stood for a moment watching the departing coach.

New London militiamen readied themselves for war. "I leave my wife the newspaper job," Matthew Green told his friend at the print shop. "Doubtless she'll do a better job than I have, but before I go I've one more issue to get out." He took his black apron from the hook. "I'll miss the smell of ink."

"Is it true that Mister Washington has been named head of it all?" Nathan asked.

Green nodded. "Continental Congress named him

general just yesterday." He reached out to pat his press. "Getting ready to print the story right now."

The next day Nathan stood on the village square with other townspeople and watched New London's militia tramp away to the sound of fife and drum. "I'll look for you when I come," he had told Matthew Green. "I'll not be far behind." He would, he thought, catch up to the militia as soon as he was released from teaching, but Nathan Hale would never again march with the militia.

Before he could give up his teaching position, a post rider brought a special letter, not to the newspaper office, but to the school. The General Assembly of Connecticut wanted him to be an officer in the Continental army. He would not be fighting alongside the New London militia. He sat that evening at his desk in the Lawrence home and turned the notice over and over in his hand.

It was an honor, this offer, and he knew he would accept. He did not, though, take up his quill and pen to answer immediately. He did not light the whale-oil lamp, either. Rather he sat in the darkening room, and he remembered. Remembered himself, a boy in short pants, playing with a hoop in the front garden. He remembered letting the hoop fall so that he could pick the small blue flowers and remembered taking those flowers to his mother.

He got up to light the lamp. In the militia men were free to come and go as they pleased. The Continental army was different. He would be enlisted for a period of years.

There would be no turning back. There was a letter to write, a commission to accept. Would his path cross that of General Washington? He thought of that night when he had met what was then only a man from Virginia. There was the story. Wasn't it about the French and Indian War? Nathan wished he had pressed to hear the story, but that evening he had not really wanted to talk to Mr. Washington, a man who spoke of war. He had believed in those days that he would never fight. Nathan folded the letter and slid it into the pocket of his waistcoat and took up his pen to consent. Doubtless if ever he did see General Washington again, there would be no time for the telling of stories.

Very soon the day came for good-byes at school. "I want you to work hard for your new master," he told them, and he found it necessary for a moment to turn his head, so that he could gaze out the window. Then he began to speak again. "I want you to learn all that is possible for you to learn. I also ask that you pray for all Connecticut men as we march to Massachusetts. We cannot stand by and watch our neighbors fall for a cause in which we too believe." He moved then to stand at the door as he had the first day that now seemed long ago, and as he had done that first day, he took each scholar's hand. He said a few words about each boy and about his hopes for the boy's future.

"You've grown tall since first we met," he said to young Timothy Green, "and you've learned much."

"I deliver papers for my mother," said Timothy. He

turned to look at the hitching post where the black horse waited. "I ride Ebony." He studied his feet, and he lowered his voice. "Some of them, you know, my friends, some say we've got to hate Jonah. I don't think so, sir, do you?"

"No," said the teacher. "We most assuredly are not required to hate Jonah or others of our neighbors who do not think as we do."

"But a soldier is required to kill them if they fight each other in battle, though. Isn't that so?" Timothy bit at his lip.

"Yes," said Nathan, "such is the truth of war."

When his boys were gone, the teacher closed the door to his schoolroom and went to the Lawrence home for good-byes and to pack his possessions. The Lawrences all followed him into the front garden. His trunk would travel later by way of a freight coach. He had now only to climb into the saddle.

He shook Mr. Lawrence's hand, hugged the boys, and bowed deeply to the ladies. "I'll write to you, Nathan," said Betsy. Her face grew red. "I mean, to keep your spirits up. Already I've written to some of the other New London boys."

Nathan felt so drawn to the lady. He did not want to leave without expressing what he felt, but he still did not know what to say. He could feel Mr. Lawrence watching. He swallowed back words about how he would miss her, and reached out to take her hand. "I look forward to those letters." He turned his gaze to include the others. "I am grateful to have shared your home and am sad to leave this spot where I have received such kindness."

Anna Myers

And so the man left New London. He was no longer a schoolteacher. He was about to become a soldier, but he had been told to first make a recruiting trip to Coventry. It would be good to see his family again, and he hoped to take some of his old friends into his regiment. Still, he knew he would be anxious to leave his father's farm. Now that he had decided to be a soldier, he wanted to get on with the job.

CHAPTER THIRTEEN

The Boy

They left Stone Croft in the late afternoon. Jonah sat on the plush red seats and stared through the window. In town he saw the undertaker driving his cart and saw the small white dog trailing after. Someone had died in New London, someone whose family could not afford the big coach to carry the body to the burial hill.

All that first night Mr. Samuel drove, and the coach bounced about on the rough roads. Little Tobias woke often and cried out into the darkness. "There, there," Miss Jayne would say to him. "Nothing will hurt my darling," but Jonah could hear the fear in her voice.

He had been given a pillow for his head, but even when the child was quiet, Jonah slept but little. The sound of the wheels on the road filled his ears. Earlier, they had stopped at a country inn. Several men sat at tables drinking ale. Mr. Samuel moved to the kitchen, calling out for the proprietor.

When a short, stout man appeared, Mrs. Samuel asked for two rooms. The proprietor said nothing. He wiped his hands on his apron and studied Samuel Hale. "Where is it you hail from?" he finally asked.

"New London."

"Going to New York?" The owner stepped closer to Mr. Samuel. "Lots of Tory scum been hightailing it to New York. You going to New York?"

Mister Samuel shifted from one foot to the other. "We need two rooms, just for the night. If you've but one, that will do as well."

"You're Tories, ain't you?" He did not wait for an answer. "We got Tories here, gentlemen," he called.

There was the sound of chairs being pushed back on the wooden floors. "We're leaving," said Mr. Samuel, and they did, backing from the room and running then for the coach. They did not stop again, and to the boy even the trees standing in the moonlight along the road seemed like enemies.

Finally, just before dawn, the coach stopped in front of a big house. "We are safe," Mr. Samuel said when he opened the door. "This is the estate of a friend."

Jonah had been dozing. He rubbed his eyes and looked out to see a large house looming in the dark. "I am a friend to Mister Townsend," Mr. Samuel said to the servant who called out for identification. "Tell him Samuel Hale and his family are in want of shelter."

In only moments the doors opened wide. A servant took the sleeping child while another went to the coach for bags. Jonah felt suddenly as if he might crumple to the floor, and it took all his will to lift his feet in order to climb the stairs to a waiting bed. When he woke in the morning, the boy discovered that he slept in a room that must have been used before by a boy. A coat that might have fit him perfectly hung from a peg on the wall. Jonah opened a wardrobe and saw other pieces of boy's clothing. He went to a window, pushed it up, leaned out, and looked about. He saw cattle in a nearby field. No other houses were to be seen.

They were, he learned in the morning, just outside the great city of New York. He learned too that Jacob Townsend's family had gone to England. "They will wait there for this ugly business to pass over. The rebels can't carry on this ridiculous fight long," Townsend said. He lowered his large body into a chair near a window, and he lifted the curtain to peer out.

"We are most grateful to you, sir," said Miss Jayne.

"You are welcome here." Jacob Townsend dropped the curtain and smiled up at the lady. "You are most assuredly welcome as long as I am able to stay." His smile changed to a frown. "Of late I've kept my loyalist ideas to myself. Still there are those who know what I've said in the past. If visitors come, mayhap it would be wise for you to stay upstairs. No reason to stir unwanted questions."

After breakfast the boy went back upstairs, wandered down the hall, and stood for a long time before the open window. He imagined men in red uniforms marching down the driveway. Mister Samuel would welcome the Redcoats, but the picture in his mind made Jonah uneasy.

He looked about the fine home. In the hallway were portraits of three children, two girls and a boy. The girls were bigger, and they stood beside the boy's chair. He held a bright ball on his lap. All were small, but Jonah felt certain he looked into the face of the boy in whose bed he slept.

He asked the chambermaid who dusted the stairway. "Yes," she said without stopping her work. "That'd be Mister William and his sisters a few years back, a fine lad he is. Fourteen, I believe, on his last birthday." She shook her head. "And now him off over the ocean, and you sleeping in his bed. The world's turned upside down, ain't it?" She kept at her dusting, not seeming to expect an answer. Jonah felt glad. He had no answers to give.

Even that first day the boy found sitting about almost unbearable. He began to do small chores, mostly outside. One late afternoon, he was splitting wood in the woodlot when Mr. Samuel joined him. "I worked hard as a youth on my father's farm in Massachusetts." He rolled up his sleeves. "Doubtless, wood splitting has not changed a great deal."

They had worked almost an hour when Jacob Townsend drove up in his coach. The driver took the coach on to the carriage house, but Mr. Townsend came to the woodlot.

Mister Samuel laid down his ax then. For a time the men talked of the weather, but then Mr. Townsend began to tell about a letter he had received from his wife. "William is most pleased with his school." He laughed. "The girls seem happiest about the parties."

"It will be a relief when I can take my family to England," said Mr. Samuel, "but it could take months to liquidate my holdings in New London. When things are more stable, I'll find suitable work in New York. Perhaps I can earn enough for our passage even before the New London funds are available. Jayne's father left us property in London."

"I wish I could help you," said Mr. Townsend.

"Nonsense." Mr. Samuel lifted his ax again. "You took us in when we had nowhere to turn. My pride would allow nothing more even were you able to give it."

More words were exchanged before Mr. Townsend moved away to go inside, but Jonah did not hear them. Nor did he continue to use his ax. His hand would have been too unstable. He moved about the woodlot gathering kindling, and his mind raced. "Take my family to England." The words repeated over and over in the boy's head. Family, he was certain, included Mercy and himself. Doubtless, Mercy would be pleased. He could not imagine that she would be parted from Miss Jayne and little Tobias now. Besides, even if his sister wanted to stay, where would they go? London? Hadn't he always wanted to see it someday? See it, yes, but to live there? The boy's bucket was full of wood chips. Without a word to Mr. Samuel, he wandered toward the kitchen door.

Next he looked for Mercy and found her in the back garden with Tobias, who played with a ball. "That's the ball from the picture," the boy said.

"What picture?" Mercy said.

"William's picture and his sisters in the hall. They live

in London now, and he goes to school there." Even to his own ears his voice sounded odd.

"Jonah." Mercy pulled him down to the bench beside her. "What is wrong? Something troubles you."

Sitting still was impossible, and he got up. "Mister Samuel plans to go to England on a ship."

Mercy laughed. "I hardly think he'd take a carriage."

"I'm serious. He said he wanted to take his family. Do you think that means us?"

"Don't worry. I know it does. Miss Jayne has assured me, we go where they go." She bounced the ball back to Tobias.

"You'd be glad of going, then?" The boy moved to the rock wall and leaned against it.

"Of course, what is there for us in the colonies?"

"I don't know." He turned to go back into the house.

"But you will go, won't you? You'd have to," Mercy called after him. "We must never be separated, Jonah, not with an ocean between us."

For two months, Jonah spent his days doing chores and tromping through the woods about the estate. He read too from Mr. Townsend's well-stocked library. Finally, word came that the British had taken New York City. "We can travel now," said Mr. Samuel, and thanking his friend profusely, he loaded his family back into the coach.

This time Jonah sat on the seat beside the driver, and his eyes grew large. The coach entered a world that he had never imagined. People were everywhere. They did not live in small cottages but rather in large buildings, apparently all together. A boy pulled a calf down the street just as a woman leaned from a window high above him and emptied a chamber pot onto his head. The boy pulled out a hand-kerchief, wiped off his face, and continued to walk. A lady balanced a covered basket on her head and called, "Hot corn, hot corn for sale!" Countless children weaved in and out among horses and carriages on the muddy streets, unmindful of more muck splashing their faces.

Jonah moved his head one way and then the other, constantly having his attention diverted to another sight. Still, through it all, he remained ever watchful. He had never been in a city. He wanted to see all there was to see. Most of all, he wanted to see the Redcoats as soon as they saw him.

CHAPTER FOURTEEN

The Man

The Hale homestead stood just outside Coventry, Connecticut. It was a big farm, almost five hundred acres, where wheat, corn, hay, and flax for linen grew. Apple trees thrived in the orchard, and herds of cattle grazed in the pastures. The house stood nestled in the pines, just off the national road that connected Connecticut to the world.

When Nathan turned from the town of Coventry and onto that road for the short ride home, he felt his muscles relax. It would be good to be back. He took his horse directly to the barn and found his brother David there, pitching hay to the other horses.

"You're home!" the boy cried, and throwing down his pitchfork, he ran to take the soldier's horse. "We didn't know you'd be here today. Did you know Samuel, Joseph, and John have marched off to Boston? I wish I could go."

Nathan reached out and playfully pulled his brother to him. "Someone has to help Father run this place. Already he is sending food and other supplies to soldiers. You are doing your part right here on the farm."

"It would be a deal more exciting to be a soldier than to be a hay pitcher," David complained.

"Well, pitch some to my horse, will you?" Nathan gave his brother a little shove, then turned to leave the barn. "I'm glad you aren't old enough to fight. The British will have Hales enough to use for targets."

In the house, his stepmother fussed over him with food and drink. "I've turkey in the kitchen," she said, "or would you like to start with bread and jam? There's a fresh batch of berry jam, just your favorite." Not waiting for an answer, she hurried out to bring him everything she had to offer.

His father sat at the big table with him while he ate. "Cousin Samuel has closed his mill and fled to New York," said Nathan.

His father made a sort of snorting sound. "Good place for him. The best spot for the likes of him. There's aplenty of his kind in that city, so they say."

Nathan was surprised to hear the bitterness in his father's voice and said so.

The older man, too full of feeling to sit, pushed back his chair and moved to the window, where he stood looking out. "I see it this way. There was a time for opinions, a time for disagreements, but now blood's been spilled. The time for opinions is gone. When his neighbors die, nary a decent man can cling to the other side."

"But Samuel is a decent man."

"Not in this house, he isn't, not when my boys, one with the very same name, go for soldiers, mayhap to die," said his father, and Nathan was glad that his little sister, Joanna, came into the room just then.

"Nathan!" she cried. "Oh, Nathan!" She ran to his chair and wrapped her arms around his neck. "You are my favorite brother and now you are home!"

"Your favorite, yea?" He laughed. "Now that is fine for my ears, but not so good of you to say, considering other brothers might hear."

Joanna shook her thick blond pigtails. "None of the others are here, save David, and he knows he isn't my favorite anything. He torments me with frogs in my bed and in all number of other ways."

"Step back," said Nathan, "and let me look at you." She did, and he studied her. "Ah, I fear boys will soon come courting."

She made a sound of disgust. "I've no interest in boys. They are, as far as I can see, disgusting creatures. I've decided I will never marry. I'll live here always. Did you know Father is going to build us a new house?" She did not wait for an answer. "Yes, that's it. I will live here always, and I will knit. I've learned quite well. I am going to make warm stockings for you, the other brothers too, but yours will be first."

"I'll wear them proudly." He went back to eating.

His father returned to the table. "Daughter, your help is wanted in the kitchen, but first bring me, please, a cup of sassafras tea." He looked at Nathan with a small smile.

"Now there's an item that might tempt a man to be a Tory. I suppose my brother's son drinks real English tea, hob-nobbing with British scoundrels as he does."

"Tell me about the new house," said Nathan.

"Oh, it's to be a grand place. Your stepmother is near out of her wits with delight. We're to start next month. We'll use part of this old place in the new, the ell, you know, and won't pull this one down until the other's done. When you've had your fill, we will go out to step off the site."

"I'm glad you'll use part of this old one," said Nathan, "because of Mother, I suppose." He looked about the room, remembering.

"Yes," said his father, "because of your sainted mother." His voice grew soft. "Seven years now, she's been gone, and it pains me still, your good stepmother notwithstanding."

"How is Grandmother Strong?"

"Hearty as ever." His father laughed. "I declare the woman could outwork me in the field were she of a mind to do so."

"I'll visit her tomorrow," Nathan said, "and take her to Mother's grave."

He did that, driving his father's shay. With his grand-mother holding to his arm, he walked through the burial ground to stand before the grave of his mother, Elizabeth Strong Hale, born 1728, died 1767.

"It all but took the life from me, losing her," said his grandmother. A shudder passed through her body. "Still in all, I've some thought these days that it might have fallen out for the best, three of her sons already gone for a soldier, and now you going too. How much chance could there be that all of you will return?" She sighed deeply. "At least this way, she's spared the sorrow of seeing you die in war."

He put his arm around his grandmother's shoulder. "If any one of us loses his life, it will be but an honor to the family. She'd have grieved, yes, but she'd have been proud too, just as you must."

Those summer days at home were good ones for him. On some he labored in the fields with his father, his brother David, and the farmhands. On others he went about the business of gathering soldiers.

One hot afternoon he swam with his childhood friend Asher Wright in what they had always called the great pond. When they were done with pulling each other under and splashing like the boys they had so recently been, they dressed, and sat on the log beneath the shade of a big sycamore, a spot with a view of the cemetery.

"I'll never forget the day your mother was buried over there." Asher used his head to point toward the graveyard.

"Aye, we were twelve years old, and my heart was split open. I remember I refused the ride home, and you walked with me."

"We've walked a goodly number of miles together, you and I," said Asher.

Nathan turned to his friend. "That's it exactly, what I've been telling you. Don't you see? We ought to go to war together."

"I just can't make it up in my mind to go." Asher bit at his lip.

"I've seven men to take with me. We leave tomorrow week."

"I've thought on it," said Asher. "Thought long and hard, but, Nathan, I don't mind admitting I am scared."

"So am I, friend." He said nothing for a moment, only stared off toward his mother's grave. "Any man who has a mind at all about him is afraid. I just try not to think about it. As the good bard said, 'Cowards die many times before their deaths; the valiant never taste of death but once.'"

"Remember, I didn't go to Yale. Who is this good bard?"

"Shakespeare, but it doesn't matter. What matters, I think, when the fighting comes is that you fight not only for your own life, but for the life of the men with you. I'd feel safer, Asher, with you beside me."

Asher laughed. "Well, it's a sure thing you'd not be afraid to fight in battle, you being doomed to hang." He gave Nathan a little push. "I always told you so." He pointed to the large brown mole on Nathan's neck. "The rope mark is still there."

"You strive to change the subject, but I won't let you. Will you go with me, Asher?"

"My mother would hate it something fierce."

"My father hates it too, but he doesn't try to stop me, nor my brothers already gone. He believes in the cause enough to feed as much of the army as he can, and he won't see the family of any soldier from Coventry go wanting."

"Do you, Nathan? I mean, do you believe way down deep in this cause?"

Nathan nodded. "I do. It took me some time, but yes, I believe in the cause. I don't believe we are fighting to make the English treat us more fairly, either; not anymore. We've gone too far already for that. We fight for independence! We just haven't said so out loud yet."

Asher stood and offered his hand to pull up his friend. "When do we leave?"

"One week from today."

Before he left for war, Nathan unpacked the trunk he had brought with him from New London. It was covered with deerskin and had been a present from his grandmother Strong when he went away to school. "Let this gift," she had said, "be in your mind as from your mother too. Oh, she was determined to see you educated. When your father arranged for Enoch to be prepared by Reverend Huntington for Yale College, she insisted he send you too."

Now Nathan stroked the smooth skin that covered the trunk. It would go with him to war. He took out some of the books he had taken with him to New London, but he left some too. One of those he left was the thin brown volume, *Cato*. On the inside cover was written in dark ink, "Given to Nathan Hale by his cousin Samuel Hale." The boy Jonah had long since purchased a new copy of the book, but somehow the teacher had forgotten his promise to give this one to him. He'd pack it now. Who knew when he might yet find a chance to keep his word?

Nathan wondered now where his cousin Samuel might be. His father felt bitterness that any kinsman of theirs should uphold the English side of the conflict, but he could not feel that resentment. He wished his cousin well.

One day, Nathan spent time with his brother Enoch, who came from a distance away where he served as a minister. Nathan waited near a window. Remembering how he had admonished Joanna for calling him her favorite brother, he smiled. He would never use the word *favorite* to describe Enoch, but he supposed it must be accurate. At least there was no disputing the word *closest.* Though Enoch was two years older, they had been treated almost as twins. When Nathan saw pictures from his childhood in his mind, those pictures always had Enoch in them.

The brothers walked the fields together, and they talked of the crops on their father's land. They picked berries together for a pie their stepmother would make, and they talked of the rattlesnake that had been in that same berry patch. "You picked up that stone and dashed in its head quick as lightning," said Nathan. "He would have gotten me for sure."

"Would that I could always keep you from such creatures," said Enoch. He tried to laugh, but the mirth was missing. It was as near as the brothers came to discussing the war. That night they lay on their backs in the front garden, just as they had as boys.

"The Connecticut sky," said Enoch. "Do you suppose the sky is as beautiful in other colonies?"

"I'm about to find out," said Nathan. "But no, I think

for me there will never be a sky so beautiful as the one we see now."

The next evening just at dusk, the man found his step-sister, Alice, sitting in the kitchen with a basket of mending. "Could we walk for a bit?" he asked, and she set her basket on the table and smiled at him. Alice had married while Nathan studied at Yale. The bridegroom was an older man who had seemed to Mr. and Mrs. Hale to be a good match. Her new husband was indeed a kind man, but he lived only three years after the marriage, so Alice returned to the home of her mother and stepfather.

When Nathan had come home at Christmas, he had noticed a change in his relationship with Alice. Gone was the totally natural relationship that had been between them when he had gone to college at fourteen and she was fifteen. Once at Christmas, he had come up behind her in the hall and reached out to pull at the dark hair she had not yet put up. His hand touched her curls, and a startling sensation went through his body. She turned to look at him then, her eyes questioning. "Your hair is lovely," he said, and without waiting for a reply he moved on.

Now they walked in the orchard. "You married once while I was away," he said.

She laughed. "And it mattered not one whit to you, did it?"

"I was but a boy then, only seventeen."

She stopped beneath a tree and looked up at him. "Are you trying to ask me something, Nathan?"

He leaned against a pear tree. "No, I have no right to

speak now, but this I will ask. Don't marry someone this time only because our parents approve. If you marry while I am away, make it someone of whom you are abundantly fond."

For a long moment their eyes met, and then slowly, she smiled. "I should be much surprised to find myself falling in love with anyone here while you are away."

A few days later, Nathan left to become a soldier. Joanna came to him on the morning of his departure with the stockings she had knit for him. "Put these in," she said, and she ran her hand over the trunk. "What a pleasant feel it has. Mayhap Grandmother will buy one like this for me one day."

"I tell you what," said her brother. "If you are a good girl, I'll buy you one when the war is over."

The next day he bade them all good-bye and rode away. He and the other men went first to Boston, ready for war, but they found that no one was fighting. Along with waiting fellow soldiers, they settled uneasily on the hills south of Boston. Looking down they could see the busy city where smoke rose from household fires, and they knew that red-coated soldiers were housed in most of those homes, unwelcome guests. To the east they could see the great ocean, its waters brimming with British ships, an indication of the mighty size of the enemy. At night, the lanterns hanging from the ships made more of a blaze than did the city, where the supply of lamp oil and other goods ran low due to the British blockade.

Nathan spent his time reading, writing letters, playing

checkers, and in athletic games with his comrades. He discovered that he could kick a ball farther than anyone else in his company. "A pity the talent won't stop one of the king's men from putting a bullet or a bayonet through me," he said to himself.

When the winter came, the soldiers knew there was little chance of action. Armies did not fight during the winter. Nathan sat in his tent while great white flakes fell from the sky, covering the encampment and the city below.

As the snow fell, Nathan, who had been made a captain now, and his brother Americans read the words of a man named Thomas Paine. His pamphlet, *Common Sense*, argued for complete separation from England. The writer claimed it was time for the thirteen colonies to form a new nation. Paine's words were reprinted in newspapers all across the provinces, and Nathan thought of young Timothy Green atop Ebony delivering Paine's message to New London.

Nathan obtained a copy of the fifty-page document, and he read parts of it to those who served under him. "The blood of those already killed calls out for independence." They stood about the fire on a cold January morning. The captain searched the faces of the shivering men. The writer was saying that ordinary people could understand and participate in government. It was an idea that pleased Nathan Hale, and he read on: "America shall make a stand, not only for herself, but for the world."

Finally, with the March thaw, the soldiers thought they were about to fight. Nathan kept a tight grip on his musket.

"We'll show the bloody lobsterbacks now," the men told one another, but Nathan worried. Some of his men did not even own proper guns.

No fighting occurred, though. The British, aware that the Americans' hillside location gave them a vast advantage, moved quietly to their ships and sailed away. Orders came down from General Washington. The American army too would move to New York City.

In New York, the officers were allowed leave occasionally. Nathan enjoyed such evenings in the taverns as much as the other officers did. He especially enjoyed the singing that sometimes broke out. His favorite song was "The Rich Lady over the Sea," and often he would stand, wave his tankard, and belt out:

There was a rich lady lived over the sea,
And she was an island queen,
Her daughter lived off in the new country,
With an ocean of water between,
The old lady's pockets were filled with gold,
Yet never contented was she,
So she ordered her daughter to pay her a tax on the tea.

The handsome young captain was always joined by others long before he got to the part about how the daughter threw the tea in the sea. Many a lady smiled especially sweetly at Nathan, but he made no move to approach such women. There was no space in his life for females now. That would have to wait.

Despite the relaxing nights out, Nathan could not be happy. It troubled him that the men he led were often hungry. They would have watery soup with a scant bite or two of vegetables or at times nothing at all. Hunger gnawed away at their insides. It especially troubled Nathan that he could see British supply ships, full of provisions.

One afternoon he studied those ships, and his spyglass fell over and over on a small sloop. Nathan could see that the ship was manned by only a few sailors, but it was moored near a huge war vessel with the name *The Asia* painted on its side. Should he try to take the small sloop? It would be a dangerous operation.

He put down his glass and thought. There was no way of knowing for certain what that small vessel contained, but the idea that it could well hold food for his men would not leave his mind. As twilight began to fall, his mind was made up, but he would not order any man to take such a risk. He called his soldiers to him. "I'm asking for only four of you," he said, "and, of course, I will go." He looked from face to face. "Who will volunteer?"

It did not surprise him to see his boyhood friend jump to his feet. He had known that Asher would be with him. Three others were only seconds behind. "Good," Nathan said. "Connecticut men are always brave." He turned his gaze to the water. "We will make our move at midnight."

Nathan went then to his own tent and stretched upon his cot. Sleep, he knew, was out of the question, but he did hope to rest. His muscles, though, were far too tense for relaxation, and his mind went to his home in Connecticut.

He could see his father, bent over his Bible. He pictured little Joanna. She had thrown herself around his neck and begged him not to leave home, and he smiled to himself. He could not forget the ladies. Two of them, he felt certain, would be pleased if he declared his desire to court them as soon as this war was over. How would he ever decide between them? One of them was bound to be left furious. Little wonder he did not fear *The Asia*'s guns.

Finally, when he held his watch near the light of his lantern, the hands read eleven forty-five. Time to go. He pushed himself up from the cot and put on his uniform. If he died, he wanted to be dressed as an officer. Before he left the tent, he dropped to his knees and asked for God's protection. Still, he knew that British soldiers also prayed to that very same God.

Few words were exchanged. Nathan led his men to a rowboat. With only the light of the quarter moon, they moved slowly and silently through the water. They were close now, close enough to smell the hint of gunpowder that hung about *The Asia*.

Nathan drew in his breath. Would that smell be the cause of his death or, even worse, the death of his men? His eyes were more accustomed now to the darkness. It seemed to him that only one man walked sentry duty.

The rowboat moved closer and closer. Now the sloop blocked *The Asia* from their view. No one stirred on the deck of the sloop. How many men were aboard? It was up to him to find out. The rowboat drew up beside the rope ladder that hung over the side of the sloop. Nathan stood up. It was necessary to leave his musket behind. With only a long knife as a weapon, he began to climb the rope.

He did not look back at his men. His eyes searched only upward, up toward the deck of the sloop. When his feet were on the next-to-the-last step, he slowly began to raise his head, just enough to see over the side. His gaze swept over the area. No one in sight! The deck was empty.

He hesitated. Surely there were men on board. His eyes fell on the small opening. Whoever manned the sloop must be below. There was no turning back now. He took in a breath, and ever so slowly he drew himself up and over the side.

Now on board, he slipped first one boot, then the other from his feet. With his knife held high, he made his way carefully toward the stairs. They were narrow and steep. There was no way he could move down them without turning his back. He started down, and then stopped. What was that sound? He waited only a second. Then recognizing the sound, he smiled. Someone snored very loudly.

He went down only far enough to see what lay below. A small lantern burned dimly in one corner of the tiny area below the deck. Two soldiers were there, one on a bunk. He lay on his back, and from his mouth came the snores.

The other man sat at a small table near the light. Before him was an open book, probably a ship's log. His body slumped forward. He had fallen asleep at his post. Ever so quietly Nathan moved back up the stairs.

He made his way silently across the deck and leaned over to his men. First he put his finger to his lips. Then he held up two fingers before motioning that two men were to come to him. Again he knew that Asher Wright would be first to his feet, joined immediately by a second man. Nathan leaned down to take up three muskets. Then the soldiers began to climb.

"Take off your boots," he whispered when the men were beside him. "Two men sleep below. We will creep down to surprise them. Then we will tie them up, gag them, and take the sloop."

All three men looked across at the huge battleship. "I'll sail her," Nathan whispered. "You can stay below with our prisoners. My hope is that even if *The Asia* sees us, she will not fire. Pray that they think the ship is being sailed for some reason by her own men."

Nathan was first to go down the steps. Asher handed down his musket. Just as the first of his men had made it halfway down, the soldier at the table stirred. He rubbed at his eyes. "What the —" Nathan thrust his musket against the soldier's head. He leaned near the man's ear to speak. "*Whisht* and mum with you," he murmured, "or else I'll splatter your brains on yonder wall." Grinning, Asher finished his descent and put his gun against the head of the sleeping Redcoat.

The men laughed as they secured the prisoners, but Nathan went back to the deck, scarcely able to breathe. They still had to sail away from *The Asia* and her guns. Staying in the shadows, he waited until the guard moved to the other side of the ship. Then he pulled in the anchor, unfurled the sail, and began to move.

The sloop sailed silently and swiftly away from *The Asia* and was almost out of range when gunfire told the soldiers that the guard had sounded an alarm. Nathan kept his head down and recited the Twenty-third Psalm aloud to himself, shouting out the lines, "Yea, though I walk through the valley of the shadow of death, I will fear no evil." He would not allow himself to think that perhaps a Redcoat on *The Asia* might at that very moment be repeating the same words of King David. He did not remember, until he had climbed down the rope ladder into the shallow water amid the cheers of his men, that he had failed to put back on his boots. "Joanna," he said aloud to his faraway little sister, "the stockings you knit me have served me well."

The sloop was well stocked, even beyond Nathan's hopes. Salted meat, barrels of flour, cooking oil, beans, corn, apples, and dried peaches enough to feed a goodly number of hungry mouths filled every corner of the small vessel. There were guns too, and powder for them. Wherever Nathan went he was cheered by soldiers.

Nathan felt a thrill he had never experienced before. He had gambled with his life and the lives of his men. He had gambled, and he had won. He had been a soldier for many months, but until that moment with the sloop and *The Asia*, he had not understood the rush that came to the soldier at such a time. "I was terrified," he told Asher later, "terrified, yet exhilarated too. Do you understand?"

"I do, Nathan," he said, forgetting that he was not to call his captain by his given name. "I understand, but pray do not let the thrill override your common sense."

On July 5, word reached the soldiers that a declaration had been signed in Philadelphia the day before. It was a declaration that stated the thirteen colonies no longer considered themselves part of England. The riders brought copies of the declaration, and once more Nathan called his men together for the purpose of reading to them. He had just read, "That to secure these rights, Governments are instituted among Men, deriving their just powers from consent of the governed," when one of his men interrupted.

"Excuse me, Captain, sir, but what does that mean?" asked the man.

"It means, Private Collins, that you and I have the right to say who will make laws for us."

"Now, ain't that fine!" shouted Collins, and all the men cheered.

That evening, Nathan was given leave again to go into the city, and so it was that he saw the statue being torn down. It was a gilded likeness of King George III sitting on a fine horse. "Only been there three years at the most, I'd say," said a shopkeeper who had come out to see what the ruckus was all about.

Nathan did not take part, but stood instead under an awning and watched as men, and even a few women, with ropes yanked at the rider while others used wedges and hammers on the base. A great cheer went up when the statue toppled. Nathan did not join the shouts of approval. He felt instead a shudder of fear. What was happening? Everything he had grown up respecting had tumbled down too. Where would it all end?

Anna Myers

He watched for a time. He could hear the sound of the chisels on metal, but he did not know what was about to happen until the head of the broken statue was lifted high on a stake.

Later that night, Nathan heard another officer say, "That statue will be melted for bullets. Our dear king George will finally do us some good. Four thousand pounds of lead for musket balls, that's what he will give us."

Nathan Hale felt glad for four thousand pounds of ammunition, but still, he wished he had not seen the statue being pulled down. He wondered where his cousin Samuel rested his head that night. "I am afraid," he said, "that behind the walls of New York homes are many who do not wish to join those celebrating in the streets, men who hate the desecration of their statue."

"It's true," said another officer. "New York is full of Tories. It will be a different scene when the British come, and they will come."

They came soon. Great numbers of troops landed on Staten Island, only miles from Washington and about one-third of his army. A terrible battle followed, and the Americans were badly beaten. Washington and his bleeding army limped back to Brooklyn Heights. The British now held most of Manhattan. The war, Nathan knew, had finally really begun.

The very next day word came to Nathan Hale that he had been handpicked by Colonel Knowlton to become part of a unit called Knowlton's Rangers, organized by Washington for special service. Nathan would be one of twenty officers. "I know you all well, not only your faces, but your records. You are an elite group," Colonel Knowlton told his officers. He also said that 130 men would be chosen to serve under them. Nathan asked that Asher Wright be one of those men.

Nathan felt pleased at the recognition, but he also felt uneasy. It was rumored that part of the job of the Rangers would include acting as spies. Spying was not an activity that appealed to Nathan Hale.

That very evening, Knowlton's officers were called to a meeting in a tent that was the colonel's headquarters. He began by telling the men what the army faced. "As if the bloody British weren't enough," Knowlton said, "they say there are Hessians too. King George has rented thousands of men from German princes for the price of seven pounds a head."

"But remember you fight for your own rights," said a voice behind them. The men turned to see General Washington. "Remember you are free men fighting for the blessings of liberty. Remember you and your descandants will become slaves if you do not fight with everything you have within you."

The tent grew absolutely still as the general moved to stand at the front. Washington said then that he must try to find out the enemy's plan of attack. He needed a spy, someone who could slip unnoticed behind enemy lines. He needed to know how many men were in the enemy camps and where they might move next. General Washington needed a spy.

The officers looked at one another. No one stepped forward. It was fine, they thought, to be a soldier, but to be a spy was not honorable. To be a spy was to lie and sneak. "Very well, then," said General Washington, and he turned to leave the tent.

When the general was gone, Colonel Knowlton spoke again. "Go back to your own tents," he said. "Think about your general's request. He needs you, and I have every faith that by this time on the morrow one of you will be ready to volunteer."

All that night, Nathan tossed about on his cot. He slept not at all until he reached a decision. Just before dawn, he slipped from his tent to watch the sun rise. He resolved to say nothing to anyone. If another man stepped up when the colonel made the appeal again, he would remain quiet and feel lucky. If no volunteer moved forward, he would do so.

Through the long day, he tried to go about his usual activities, drilling his men, eating his meals with other officers, reading from *Cato*. When the sun was down, he walked toward headquarters with a heart that beat fast.

"Well," said Colonel Knowlton, "you have had time to think. Who among you will do General Washington's bidding?"

Again the tent was wrapped in silence. Nathan turned his head, trying to see as many faces as possible. *Let one of them volunteer. Let one of them volunteer.* The words echoed over and over in his mind, but no man moved.

Colonel Knowlton cleared his throat and opened his

mouth. Nathan wondered what the colonel would say, but he did not wait to see. "I will go," he said. "I will do anything General Washington wishes me to do."

The colonel smiled. "So," he said, "the youngest of you, it seems, is the bravest."

Or the most foolish, thought Nathan, but he said nothing. His fellow officers cheered, and then silently they filed out of the tent. "General Washington has asked that I bring any volunteer to him," said the colonel, and Nathan nodded.

The general sat at a table beside a lantern. As they entered he looked up, but in that second before the general became aware of his visitors, Nathan saw the leader's unguarded face. He saw the weariness that made deep lines. He saw the sadness in those blue eyes. Nathan felt glad he had volunteered. He would do anything to ease the burden that General Washington bore.

"I have a volunteer for you," said the colonel, and he reached to put a hand on Nathan's shoulder.

The general stood and put out his hand. "Captain Hale," he said. Then he turned to the colonel. "I made this fine young man's acquaintance back in New London." He sighed. "It seems a very long time ago, but I suppose it has really been little over a year." He looked back at Captain Hale. "I had a feeling then that our paths would cross again."

After Colonel Knowlton had left, Nathan reminded the general of their conversation. "You told me that should we meet in the future, you would tell me a story from the French and Indian War."

The general laughed. "So I did," he said. "Sit down first." He indicated a chair across the table from him. "It is a story about an Indian chief who came to me a few years ago. His talk hearkened back to a battle in which I had taken part as a young colonel during the French and Indian War. He told me that he had singled me out to his men and told them to be sure they killed the young leader. For two long hours we fought, their shots whizzing constantly past my head. The chief told me when we met that he said to those who fought that day, 'Mark you tall and daring warrior . . . a people yet unborn will hail him as the founder of a mighty empire.' I smiled at him then and thought it only an interesting story. Now I feel he may be right." The general reached across the table to lay his arm on Nathan's. "I tell you now that when I met you, something called out to me that I should mark the tall young man before me. I felt certain even then that an important job waited for you."

A lump had moved into Nathan's throat, and he felt unable to speak. He nodded his head, and the general took out maps. There were plans to be laid.

When Nathan went back to his tent, he found his friend Asher waiting for him. "So," he said, "is my secret out already?"

"Only I was told. One of your fellow officers came to me and told me the story. He thought someone should talk you out of the decision, and he felt I might have the best luck."

"Why would you want to make me change my mind?"

Asher began to pace. "You are far too honest to make a good spy. You do not have a dishonest bone in your body. You will be detected, Nathan, and you know what happens to a spy who is detected. You are made for honorable work, not for sneaking."

Nathan shook his head. "Don't trouble yourself over my doing dishonorable work. If any work is necessary to a great cause, it becomes honorable. I am needed, Asher, and my mind is made up."

Nathan stayed busy all the next day. He was given a suit of plain brown clothing and a broad-brimmed hat to match. His cover story was one that he could easily assume. He was to go among the enemy as a schoolmaster looking for work. He was to keep his ears open always and to make drawings of what he saw, men and artillery.

His trunk would be left behind with his friend Asher. Inside he put the things he wanted taken to his family should he not return. "Tell them Joanna is to have the trunk, and this," he said to his friend, as he picked up a small volume. "This copy of *Cato* should go to one of my former students. Give it to a boy named Jonah Hawkins if ever you should be able to find him."

"You can give it to him yourself, one day," said Asher.

Nathan laughed. "So have you changed your mind? Do you think now it might be possible for me to return?"

"I do."

"Pray tell me why. What fact is there today that makes you see things differently from last night?"

Asher turned his face away before he spoke. "I believe

now that you will return because there is nothing I can do to dissuade you from going." His voice broke for a second. "Quite simply, I believe you will return because I cannot bear to believe otherwise."

When the sun went down, Asher walked for a ways with his friend, and then Captain Nathan Hale slipped away into the darkness.

CHAPTER FIFTEEN

The Boy

Jonah had lived in New York now for a week. Mister Samuel had used almost all his money to secure two rooms in a modest inn and tavern, where both the boy and his sister were glad to be given jobs in exchange for food. Mister Samuel went out at once and soon returned with the happy announcement that he had found work as a pay clerk for the British army.

"Are you to be a soldier, then?" Miss Jayne's voice was full of alarm.

"No, the army has no need of another gentleman soldier. What they need is someone who can count out money for those they have. I've taken the soldier's oath of loyalty to the king in all my actions, but I'll not be in uniform." Jonah saw him look about the room where they had gathered for his news. No carpet covered the floor. One bed and one washstand almost filled the small space. The boy knew it seemed greatly inferior to the Hales. "Soon we will be able to afford better living quarters, and when our funds come through either from New London or from England, we will leave this wretched land behind."

Jonah, standing beside the room's one window, looked out onto a dirty alley. So far he was not impressed with the great city called New York, but he could not believe that Mr. Samuel spoke so easily of leaving America altogether. He could feel his sister's eyes boring into his back.

Mercy worked in the kitchen, and Jonah waited the tables, filled mostly with British soldiers. On his first day he was sent by the proprietor, Mr. Watson, on an errand to bring beef from the butcher. He stepped out the door with an uneasy feeling. On the carriage ride he had noticed groups of rough-looking boys standing about on street corners. Once he had even seen such a gang chasing a poor boy, who ran in front of Mr. Samuel's horse, barely escaping being run down.

He had no wish to encounter such a mob. He leaned from the inn door, his eyes searching one way and then the next. He let go the breath he had not realized he held. Only men and women moved along the street. He had not gone far, though, before a voice called to him, "Boy, you there! Wait up!"

Jonah sucked in his breath. Should he run? He threw a quick glance over his shoulder. Five boys had just rounded the corner behind him. They were dirty, ragged, and mean looking. Jonah broke into a run. He felt his hat fall from his head, but he did not slow down. He dashed around two ladies and bolted around a corner, running smack into a large man. "Mind your step, you little bugger!" the man yelled, but Jonah ran on even though he no longer saw the gang behind him.

Finally he saw the sign with the painted pig, the butcher's shop. He yanked at the door with a bell above it and flung himself into the empty shop, where he leaned against a large barrel and caught a bit of breath. A man in a stained white apron came from the back.

Jonah pulled himself up. "I'm Mister Watson's boy," he said, "and I am sent for his order of beef."

"I'll wrap it," said the man, and he turned back to the rear room.

Just then the bell sounded again, and Jonah turned back to see a boy with a hat in his hand. "Here, Jonah," the boy said. "I brought your hat to you."

Jonah stared. "Thomas? Thomas Allen? Where did you come from?"

Thomas laughed. "I come from chasing after you."

"You were with that group that chased me?"

"I was. Didn't know at first 'twas you, and when I found you out, I yelled your name. You didn't slow, though, not even when you lost this." He held out the hat.

"Why do you run with so rough a bunch? There's no good in such a thing."

Thomas lowered his gaze. "It's a different world here in New York." He looked up. "There's suspicion everywhere. For the most part there's no work to be had. Lads spend their time standing about and trying to pick up what we can."

"Seems to me you spend your time chasing innocent boys."

Thomas shrugged. "There's plenty of rebels hereabouts, and they ain't innocent, Jonah. You'll see. Did you know my grandfather's house got burned before we left New London? We've nothing left us."

"I know," said Jonah. "I've got a job in an inn. If you want, I'll see if Mister Watson needs another boy."

Thomas shook his head. "Why should I work for hours in some inn when I can take things from rebels? Their kind took all from me and my family, didn't they?" He laughed in a strained way. "Thank you kindly, but I'll stick with my loyalist boys." He backed away, turning just to open the door. "Look about for me if you decide to join us."

"I heard the bell," said the butcher when he came in carrying a large package of meat. "Did a customer not want to wait?"

"No customer," said Jonah. "Just a boy returning my hat that blew off my head."

"A doer of good deeds, then. Glad to hear it. This city can use every bit of kindness we can get." The butcher handed the boy a package of meat.

Jonah did not correct the butcher, who thought a kind fellow had been in his shop. He thanked the man and left the building. He walked back to the inn with watchful eyes and determined he would go out only when he absolutely had to do so. Mercy looked closely at him when he went into the kitchen with the meat. "What's happened to you?" she asked. "You're all askew. Have you been running?"

He dropped the meat on the cook table. "No," he said. "I don't know what you're talking about," but when the cook went for more potatoes and a drink of ale from the cellar, he told her the truth. "I was chased by a group of rough Tory boys. Thomas Allen from home was among them."

"You were chased by Tory boys?" She put her rolling pin down hard. "Why did you not but tell them that you too support the king?"

He leaned against the table and crossed his arms. "They gave me no chance to tell them anything." Jonah scowled at his sister. "Besides," he said, "I've never declared myself a Tory."

She reached for the broom that leaned in the corner beside her. "You've been educated by a Tory these many months. You've been fed by a Tory and sheltered by a Tory. Pray tell me, when do you plan to decide whether or not you are one too?" She thrust the broom in his direction. "If you can't decide, I've no wish to see you in this kitchen."

Jonah grabbed up his apron and went out into the tavern. Two British officers sat at a table. One read from a newspaper. He put it down and said to his friend, "It says here that the Americans' Congress sent a letter they call an olive branch directly to the king, asking for peace. It said that's what they did before they voted for independence."

"How so?" The other soldier laughed and slapped his hand on the table. "I daresay the ignorant colonials were wishing for that olive branch when we pounded them a good one out on Long Island."

The man who had held the paper spotted Jonah. "There you are, boy. Make haste with you! We're in need of two tankards of ale. Our throats are as dry as the dusty streets of this dread city were before yesterday's rain."

Jonah moved to fill their order, all the time studying the men. He knew now how to recognize officers by the fancy decoration on their sleeves. He had heard that Master Hale was a soldier now, an officer in the opposing army. How did his uniform look?

Jonah did not know that his schoolmaster walked the same streets he did. He did not know that his uniform had been changed for a disguise. Mercy saw him first, and she ran to the small room she shared with her brother. Jonah sat up from where he had been stretched on his narrow bed when she came rushing in, full of the story.

"It was him, as sure as I'm standing before you," she declared when the boy expressed doubts. "I guess I know Master Hale when I see him. I was his student too!" She plopped down on her own bed. "He's left the American army. Says he wants no part of them, wants instead to be a schoolmaster again. Isn't that grand?" She smiled and leaned back on her pillow. "He took my hand and kissed it." She sighed deeply. "Can you believe it? He asked me to tell no one, and you must not repeat this." Her voice lowered. "Miss Jayne and Mister Samuel must never hear." She smiled and sighed again. "Master Hale says he will have much to tell me when this terrible mess is over. He leaned real close to me and touched my hair. He fancies me, Jonah! Can you believe it? Master Nathan Hale all smitten with the likes of me?"

Jonah certainly could not believe it. Why would Master Hale leave the American army? Why would he suddenly be kissing Mercy's hand and making advances toward her? He said nothing more to his sister, but he determined to be ever watchful.

It was only a few day later he caught a glimpse of a man in a brown suit. Jonah was some distance behind and carrying a large market basket. At first it was only the brown suit, but then he realized he recognized the movements. The man who had just rounded the corner was Master Hale. Jonah was certain of the fact.

He followed, just in time to see the brown-suited man go into a tavern. Master Hale was already at a table when Jonah burst through the door. The man dropped his eyes and pulled the brim of his hat low. Jonah wanted to dash to his table. He wanted to blurt out a hundred questions. Instead, he waited, staying close to the entrance. Yes, it was certain. His Yale-educated teacher sat at a table in New York City, dressed as a simple country man.

Jonah moved slowly to the teacher's table. When he put his hand on the table, the man looked up. He smiled slightly, but his eyes were sad. "Hello, Jonah," he said. "Won't you sit with me?"

Jonah pulled out the chair and sat down. He put his basket on the floor beside him, but he said nothing. There were too many questions racing through his mind. He did not know where to start.

"Mercy told you, I suppose. I mean, about seeing me?"

"She did. She thinks you fancy her." He glared at the teacher.

The teacher looked uncomfortable. "I'm sorry." He lifted his hands in a helpless gesture. "I hated to trifle with her that way, but I was desperate to keep her quiet. If she talks about me, or if you do, I could be arrested."

"Arrested?" Jonah's voice was loud.

"*Shush*!" The teacher leaned toward the boy. "I'm a spy, Jonah, a spy for General George Washington."

"A spy?" The boy stared at the teacher. A spy was dishonest. A spy was a liar! Hadn't the teacher talked to him about how lies of omission were still lies? Now that same man was lying to everyone, even to Mercy, a poor girl whose heart he played with as if it were a toy.

"Would you like something to eat, Jonah? Or maybe you'd like some cider?"

Jonah said nothing. A great rage was growing inside him. Suddenly this man, the man sitting quietly at this table, seemed a symbol for all the bad things that had happened. Oh yes, he had scolded Jonah for lying, but now everything about him was a lie. Jonah stood abruptly and pushed back his chair, pushed it so hard it toppled and went skidding across the floor. "You are a base man," he said in a low, hate-filled voice, "a liar and a sneak thief. I hope I never have to look upon your face again." He ran then. The boy ran from the tavern, and he did not take his basket.

Outside, he did not turn back toward the inn or to the market. Where would he go? He didn't want to see anyone. He had no wish to explain what had happened or why he did not have a basketful of vegetables. He would walk. After a very long time, he would go back for the basket. Master Hale would be gone by then. He would be off doing whatever dirty work that must be done by spies.

Jonah brushed roughly at his eyes when he felt the tears. He would not cry. He had not cried for a very long time. The more he tried to hold back the tears, the more they pushed to come out. All at once, the dam broke, and he was sobbing by the time he ran into the men.

First he saw the soldiers. Then through his blurred vision, he became aware that Mr. Samuel stood before him. "What goes here?" Mister Samuel reached out to stop Jonah, who had tried to push around him. "You chaps go on. I'll just be a moment."

Jonah did not want to say anything, but the words came tumbling out. "He's a spy. Master Hale's disguised himself as a country schoolmaster, but it is a lie! It is all a lie, everything about him."

"You saw my cousin? You saw Nathan Hale?" Mister Samuel pressed hard against the boy's arm.

Jonah nodded. "I did." He wiped at his eyes with the back of his hand. He was calmer now. "He doesn't want anyone to know. He wants to keep it a secret."

"As well he might." Mister Samuel had a look on his face, an expression that made him seem far away. "You go back to the inn, Jonah," he said, "and don't trouble your-self concerning my cousin."

"I must return for my basket and then go to the market."

"Very good. You do just that." Mister Samuel stared off into the distance far over Jonah's head.

CHAPTER SIXTEEN

The Man

For a little more than a week Captain Nathan Hale, dressed as a schoolmaster, moved among the British. He drew diagrams, wrote down locations, and made estimates as to the number of British soldiers, then hid those papers away.

Finally, he was ready to go back to his camp. Climbing from the ferry, he had barely taken a step when suddenly, from he knew not where, two Redcoats were upon him, each one grabbing an arm. "You are under arrest," one of them said to him, "by order of General William Howe."

The soldier's heart seemed to drop. "What is the charge?" he asked.

"Spying," answered one of the Redcoats, and he spat at Nathan's shoe. First they tied his hands behind him, and then they shoved him roughly onto the bed of a wagon. Nathan lay on his back on the rough wood, trying to ignore the musket barrel jabbed into his ribs. He stared up at the stars that twinkled above New York City and knew those same stars were shining over Connecticut.

He was taken to the Beckman mansion, a stately home, recently made headquarters for General Howe. "Out with you." The musket pushed harder against his side. Nathan moved his feet against the wagon bed and managed to slide to the end, where he could get out.

Nathan was taken to the back door of the mansion, where two Redcoats stood on either side of the entry. "Got him, I see," said one of the guards. "Give you any trouble?"

"Not a whit," said one of the captors, and this time he poked at Nathan with a bayonet.

"Take him on in," said the guard. "The word is Howe wants to question the yokel his ownself."

"I'd reckon things must go slow with the war if he ain't got better ways to pass his evening than with this pumpkin." The bayonet pushed the soldier forward.

The general sat at a writing table near a window. He looked up as the soldier was shoved into the room. He leaned forward. "Name?"

"Nathan Hale"

"Why are you in New York?"

"I seek a position as a schoolmaster." He touched his haversack. "My diploma from Yale College is in my bag."

The general waved his hand in a gesture of dismissal. "We know who you are and why you are behind our lines." He turned to the Redcoat guard. "Take his shoe and rip off the sole."

The guard did as he had been told. Pieces of folded

papers fell from the shoe, and he handed them to the general, who looked at them and then at the soldier. "I ask again, who are you?"

The prisoner drew in a deep breath. "Captain Nathan Hale of the Continental army."

"Now tell me what you were doing out of uniform behind our lines."

The soldier looked straight into the general's eyes. "I have been on an information-gathering mission for General Washington."

"You are a spy, and as such you will be hanged." The general took up a sheet of paper and wrote on it briefly. "Take him to Provost Marshal Cunningham. He will be confined to the greenhouse tonight, and executed at eleven on the morrow."

Cunningham was a big man whose sneer matched his cold eyes. "Untie his hands," he told the guards. "Can't sleep all tied like that." He laughed. "Want him to rest well, we do."

Nathan rubbed his wrists where the ropes had left burns. "May I speak with a minister?"

Cunningham shook his head. "Nah, why would a God-fearing man want to waste his time with the likes of you?"

"May I at least have a Bible, then, and some writing paper and pen?"

Cunningham stuck his face close, and Nathan smelled liquor on his breath. "Ain't got no Bible, no paper or pen, and ain't got no interest in finding one."

"I've got a Bible, sir, and some paper," said one of the guards. "I could fetch it."

"I said no!" Cunningham shouted, and he stomped away. He turned back to leer at the guard. "Are you questioning my decisions, Smith?"

"No, sir," said the guard, and his face looked sad. When the marshal had rounded the corner, the guard spoke to Nathan. "There's a water bucket with a dipper in the corner and some hay if you're of a mind to make something of a bed." He stepped outside the glass room and took his place in front of the door.

And so Nathan was alone. There was no way that sleep would ever come to him, but he would, he thought, make himself as comfortable as possible while he waited for daylight. He went to the hay, undid the binding, and spread it in layers on the hard floor. With his fingers laced together behind his head, he lay down on his back. For a time he thought about the execution. Would they give him a chance to speak? If the opportunity came, what would he say? He smiled. It mattered but little he supposed. He didn't know if anyone would listen, and they certainly wouldn't remember. Still, those would be his last words on earth. They mattered to him. He began to go over lines from literature that he had committed to memory. *Cato*! He would use the speech Cato made when he saw his son's body. No, he would paraphrase; put the speech in his own words.

His mind went then to his family, and to his friends. He did not want to think of how his death would pain them. Instead, he would close his eyes and picture each one in his mind. His thoughts went to his father standing in a field, his scythe in his hand. Next, he saw Enoch standing behind a pulpit with his Bible and Joanna busy with a knitting needle, Alice walking in the orchard. Nathan felt his muscles relax, first in his arms and shoulders, then down through his body. He slept.

Then he saw her, a tall woman in a long flowing white dress, and she moved slowly toward him. The soldier shook his head and rubbed at his eyes. Was he dreaming? He wasn't sure. It was too dark to see her face, but something about her movements was familiar. "Nathan," she said to him, and he knew.

"Mother?" He started to sit up, but she was beside him now, on her knees. Her hand on his shoulder held him gently back. "Just rest now," she said. "I've come to be with you."

"I'm sorry, Mother," he said. "I know you insisted Father send me with Enoch to be educated. Now all that education will be wasted."

The woman shook her head. "Oh no, my sweet boy, nothing about you was wasted, all those minds, all those boys you touched."

Her words made him think. "There was a boy, a boy named Jonah. I think he might be the reason—"

"*Shush*." She put her finger to her lips. "It does not matter now. Soon you will understand so much. Sleep, sweet Nathan, sleep." She bent, touched his cheek, and kissed him on the forehead. Then she was gone.

"Mother!" he said. He sat up and looked around. He was alone in the greenhouse. Had he dreamed his mother's presence? He could still feel her touch on his cheek and her kiss on his forehead. He lay down and went to sleep.

They brought him mush and bread for breakfast, but he did not eat. He washed his face by pouring water into his hands and splashing his face. He combed his hair with his fingers and retied the cloth that held it back. His hands did not shake. His heart did not race. He felt removed already from the greenhouse and from the soldiers that guarded him, as if somehow he were above it all and looking down at himself.

His watch had been taken from him, but he knew from the position of the sun that it was early when they opened the door and ordered him out. "Did they change the time?" the soldier asked.

"No," said the guard, "I don't think they have." The guard had changed during the night. This one had a softer voice and a red blotch on his cheek.

Another guard joined them. "Earl," said the first guard, "I wonder why they want him so early."

"It's a two-mile march and besides, I reckon someone wants him to have to watch while they get things ready." He carried a rope. "Put your hands behind your back, rebel," he said. "I get the job of tying them up for you."

When next the guard with the red blotch spoke, he lowered his voice. "Don't think they will make him beg or nothing if that's what they are thinking. He ain't going to make no scene, I'll wager, not this one." He shifted his musket from one shoulder to the next. "I'd like to skip this duty, I would."

Spy!

It was a pleasant September day with just a hint of fall in the breeze. Under different circumstances, Nathan would have much enjoyed the walk. Still interested in what he saw about him, he noticed the great smoke rising from a different part of the huge city. A fire of considerable size must have raged there.

"Halt!" said one of the soldiers after they had marched some distance and were in the military park. "We got to wait here for the cart."

Nathan wondered for a moment why they needed a cart. Oh, of course, they would stand him on a cart, and then they would drive it from beneath him. His eyes fell on an army tent. A man wearing a uniform came out of the tent and walked toward them. "I am John Montresor, aide-de-camp to the general. How is it that you stop here with the prisoner?"

"Orders, sir," said the guard. "We was told by Provost Marshal Cunningham to wait here for him and the cart."

John Montresor studied the soldier. "Let the prisoner come into my tent. The poor fellow should be allowed to sit at least."

"We got orders," said the guard.

"I will take responsibility," said Montresor. He reached out, took Nathan by the arm, and led him into the tent. "Sit down, my boy," he said when they were inside.

Nathan saw paper and a pen on a table. "Please, sir," he said. "I wonder if I might be allowed to write a few words to my brother to say good-bye and to my commander, Colonel Knowlton, to apologize for my failure."

"Let me untie your hands." He looked at his watch. "I'm afraid you've not much time."

With the pen in his hand, Nathan wasted no time. "Dear Brother Enoch," he wrote. "I want you to know that I suffer no fear while I wait to die. I did what I thought was right, knowing full well the consequences should I be caught. I send you my love, and ask you to convey it also to Father and the others. Part of me is, I think, already on the other side, and I can tell you, dear brother, that I am at peace. Until we meet again, Your Brother, Nathan."

On the other piece of paper he wrote, "Colonel Knowlton, My assignment ended with capture. Forgive me my failure."

John Montresor stood. "Cunningham has arrived. Here he comes."

Nathan quickly signed the note and folded it. Then he stood, turned his back, and put his hands in position to be tied.

Provost Marshal Cunningham came storming into the tent. "I'll take charge of the rebel now." He reached out to grab at Nathan's arm. Then he saw the letters. "What's this?" he demanded.

Before Nathan could speak, Cunningham snatched up the papers. "Wrote letters, did you?"

"Yes, he did," said John Montresor. "I can see to them."

"No need. I'll take care of them." Cunningham shoved the notes into the pocket of his uniform jacket.

They will never be delivered, thought Nathan. "Thank you

for your kindness," he said to the aide-de-camp, and then he stepped out of the tent.

Cunningham swung his heavy body onto the back of a horse. In addition to the cart there was a third Redcoat with a rope around his neck, and a drummer boy, who began to play. "Here." The man with the rope lifted it from his neck. "Bend down here, rebel. You get to carry your own rope." He settled the coil around Nathan's neck.

"Move it now," jeered one of the guards, and he pushed at Nathan with a bayonet.

They stopped beneath the apple tree. Nathan climbed onto the cart, and he looked down at the faces in front of him. There was aide-de-camp Montresor with a tear on his cheek. The soldier with the red blotch on his face also wiped at tears. *They are good men*, thought Nathan. Just before he was asked if he had last words, his eyes fell on the boy Jonah. Nathan wanted to say something, wanted Jonah not to suffer over his death, but there was no time to think. He smiled briefly at Jonah and then said the words he had planned. "I only regret that I have but one life to lose for my country." Then he had the thought that *he* wanted to decide the moment of his end. He did not wait for the soldiers to move the cart. Instead, he stepped off. Just before everything went black, he saw her again. His mother floated before his eyes, and she motioned him to her.

CHAPTER SEVENTEEN

The Boy

Night came and still Jonah huddled on the rock, but finally he pulled himself up. He had to see. He had to go back to that apple tree. He turned to look at the city behind him. Where was the place? He couldn't even remember what they called it. Oh yes, Artillery Park; that was it. He started to walk.

On the dark streets, it was not easy to find someone who could direct him. First he asked an older man who had a chicken tucked under one arm. The man looked at the boy for a moment, then waved his free arm and broke into a string of words in some foreign language. Jonah ran on.

Next he tried a woman with a basket of bread. She shook her head when asked about Artillery Park. "I'd not be knowing," she said, "but I do know a boy like you ought not be running amok at night, not with the world gone crazy."

"Thank you, ma'am," he said, and moved away.

"Wait," she called. "You've the look of hunger. Take this."

He turned back to see her tear a hunk of bread from one of her loaves and hold it out to him. The boy had no desire to eat, but he knew that he would later. He grabbed the bread. "Thank you, ma'am," he said again. He shoved the bread into the pocket of his waistcoat, and then he ran.

Finally, he found a man who could tell him how to get to Artillery Park. "Thataway," he said, and he pointed, " 'bout a mile, I'd say. Heard a fellow met his Maker there today, a spy, I reckon."

Jonah looked at the man. He had never seen him before, would never see him again. He could say the words that were splitting him into pieces. "I caused it," the boy said. "It is my fault he's dead, and they won't take him down."

"What are you talking about, boy? Are you out of your head?"

Jonah did not answer. He walked away. Now that he was close, he did not run. He walked and tried to plan.

At the park, he found the rock wall and followed it to the apple tree. Since the morning, a small camp of soldiers had appeared nearby. One armed Redcoat leaned against the tree. The body still swung there, but he could not let his gaze linger in that direction. Desperately, he had hoped there would be no guards. How could he possibly get the body down?

For a long time, he stared at the soldiers, at the horses tethered on the other side of the tents, and at their fires.

Finally, he moved away, careful to keep behind the wall until he was out of sight of the camp. He knew the way back to the inn from the park, and he walked in that direction. He could, he knew, at this time of night get into the room he shared with Mercy without being seen. He could then sleep in comfort and go about his business in the morning. "No," he said aloud. "I'll not sleep again in a bed paid for by him."

Finally, he saw an alcove sheltering stairs that ran along the outside of an elaborate ladies' hat shop. Exhausted, Jonah threw himself into a corner, and resting his head against one of the lower steps, he slept fitfully, waking often to check for dawn.

At first light, he was up and moving. Outside the kitchen, he eased the door open ever so slightly. There was the cook, busy at the stove. Mercy stood nearby at a table, kneading bread. Slowly, he reached through the opening toward her arm. When he touched her, she jumped, but she made no sound. He closed the crack, backed slightly away, and waited.

In only a moment, she came. "Jonah," she said and her voice shook. She reached for him, and her fingernails cut into his arm. "Where have you been? I was near out of my head with worry." She looked over her shoulder. "I can't stay out here long. I told her I had to use the outhouse."

"They killed him, Master Hale, I mean. They hanged him for a spy."

She looked down at her feet, and she nodded. Tears ran down her cheeks. "I knew you'd hate it something awful. We all do."

Spy!

A hard little laugh escaped Jonah's lips. "We? Do you mean Mister Samuel?"

Mercy leaned closer, almost touching his nose with hers. "Yes, of course Mister Samuel and Miss Jayne, me too. Our hearts are broken. Mister Samuel looks like a dead man himself."

Jonah laughed again. "It's his fault, his and mine. I told Mister Samuel, and he turned him in. Soldiers told me he was betrayed. It had to be Mister Samuel. Do you hear me, Mercy?" He was yelling now. "He betrayed him, his own flesh and blood."

Mercy shook her head. "No, are you sure?"

"I am, and, Mercy, I hope never to see the man again."

She dropped his arm then and her hands flew to cover her face. "Don't say such, Jonah! He's taking us to England." She looked at him then, her face gone white. "Only just now at his breakfast table, he told me. 'Mercy,' he said, 'I've found the means for travel. We leave for London tomorrow. Where do you suppose Jonah has gone off to? We have to find him. We want him with us too, of course.' That's what he said, Jonah, and you talking of never seeing him again!"

He drew in a deep breath. "He's in there now, is he?"

"Yes, like I said, eating."

"I've changed my mind," he said, and he turned to the door. "I've a need to see his face." He reached for the door and marched through the kitchen.

The cook looked up from her stove. "Well, there you are!" she called. "You're a cheeky thing, running off and leaving customers wanting!"

Jonah, striding through the kitchen and into the dining room past her, did not even turn in her direction. Mister Samuel sat alone. An empty plate before him, he leaned back in his chair and smoked a pipe, not seeing Jonah until the boy stopped directly before him and shouted, "You betrayed him!" He pounded with his fist on the table. "You turned him in, and now he's dead!"

"Jonah . . ." Mr. Samuel stood up and laid down his pipe. "Jonah, I am employed by the British army. I've taken an oath. Many English soldiers' lives could have been lost." He covered his face with his hands, and there were sobs in his voice. "Oh God, Jonah, you can't hate me more than I hate myself. Yet what else could I do?" Now he only whispered. "What action did you expect when you told me?" He took his hands from his face and held them palm up and open. "Please, Jonah."

"No!" The boy backed away from the table. "We both of us killed him. You're no worse than me, but I'm done with you and all them like you. I'll find me a gun, and I'll fight you! I will." He turned then to run. Mister Samuel made no attempt to stop him. Mercy, who had followed him into the dining room, reached out for him, but he brushed her off.

Outside the kitchen door, he leaned against the back wall and waited, his breaths coming quickly. He knew his sister would come to him, and she did, tears streaming down her face.

"Jonah," she pleaded. "Please don't go off like this. You're too young to fight. They won't let you. Can't you see how miserable Mister Samuel is over what happened? Please go with us to England. Remember Father's stories about living there?" She choked back a sob. "There's no place for us here, and we can't be separated."

"No, Mercy, I can't go to England, not now." He reached out to put his arm around her shoulder and draw her close. "I don't find fault in your going. I'll come to you someday, or you to me."

"How would we ever find each other again? Please, Jonah, don't refuse without more thought. We leave on the morrow about ten. Please come. Mister Samuel will welcome you still. I'm certain of it."

Jonah released his sister and turned his face away from her. He had no wish to distress her before it became absolutely necessary, but he knew he would not be sailing to London, not anytime soon. "I'll come to you in the morning, no matter what decision I reach."

"What will you do now?"

He shrugged. "He's hanging there still on that apple tree. I wonder, does Samuel Hale know that? I cannot bear that, Mercy. I tell you, I can't."

"But what can you do? You are but a boy, Jonah!"

"I'll find a way to get him down," he said, and he turned to move away.

"Wait," she said, "are you hungry?"

Suddenly he was. He stuck his hand into his pocket. The bread he had stored there had turned to crumbs. "I won't go back inside there. He might come upon me."

"I'll bring you a plate." She disappeared quickly and

came back with a plate loaded with eggs, meat, and bread. She also carried a tankard of cider, and under one arm she held an apple.

"I've got to go back to work," she said when she handed him the plate. "Promise me you will come with us, and promise you'll not do anything dangerous. You might consider that you're all I have."

"I'll see you at the ship," he said, and he took the plate, sat on an overturned keg, and began to eat. He could feel Mercy still looking at him, but he kept his eyes down. After a time she went back into the kitchen. When the last bite was gone, he set the plate and tankard beside the door.

A thought had come to him while he ate, and now he walked the streets of New York looking for a gang of hoodlums, the Tory boys who ran with Thomas Allen. He had not searched long until he saw them coming around a corner, Thomas and three other boys, slightly ahead. "Thomas," the boy shouted. "Thomas Allen, wait for me!"

All four of the boys turned to look, two with arms folded across their chests. Jonah felt no fear. Doubtless he would feel nothing even if they beat him. He walked close. "Thomas," he said, "will you talk with me? I'll keep you but a few minutes."

"It's the fellow from home," said Thomas. "Leave us be, and I'll catch up to you later." Casting angry looks at Jonah, the other three sauntered away.

"It's Master Hale," he said. "They hanged him up from a tree, and now they won't take him down."

"Are you daft?" He shook his head. "I don't believe you. Why would anyone hang Master Hale?"

Jonah stared down at the muddy street. "He was a spy."

"Master Hale wouldn't do that!"

"He did." Jonah looked up at his friend. "He believed he should do anything for his cause. Now they've made an example of him, Thomas. It's awful. I want to cut him down."

"Aren't they watching him?"

"They are, but listen, if we could get a horse, you could get the guard to chase you—"

"*Whoa*, now!" Thomas held up his hands. "I am sorry about Master Hale. He was a good man, no matter his rebel ideas, but I don't see the good in risking our lives. None of it's our fault, is it?" He walked away.

"Thomas—"

"You'd best forget it, Jonah," Thomas called over his shoulder, and then he was gone. Jonah stood for a while staring ahead. Then he began to walk. For a time he wandered aimlessly, but he knew he would go there, behind that rock wall. He stayed most of the day, watching, leaving only long enough for a trip to a well for a drink of water, and to walk in an alley until he found a shed with a shovel. He took it and went back to the park. Soon he was back behind the wall, where he stayed the rest of the day.

He stayed long after the darkness came, and he studied the tree and the guard, who was changed once during the time he watched. He could climb that tree and use his knife to cut the rope. He would need a blanket under the tree, so the body would fall on it, and he would need a horse. So lost was he in his thoughts that he did not notice Mercy until she was almost beside him. "Jonah," she whispered. "Jonah, please come away with me. I promised Father to keep you safe from the whale."

He shook his head. "It's too late. I've been swallowed, Sister. I'm in the belly of the whale, but I intend to see Master Hale put in a decent grave. I aim to filch a horse." He pointed with his head in the direction of the camp. "There's some tethered over there, and I can take a blanket from a tent."

"You'll be caught, but even if you were to escape capture, what of the guard?"

"Look at him, his musket against that tree. I'll come from behind him and grab up the gun. I'll make him help me."

"You'll not sneak up on him with a horse."

The boy sighed. "Doubtless you are right. I've got to think."

"I'll help you, Jonah. I'll get his attention while you snatch the gun. Then we'll make him cut Master Hale down. I'll hold the gun on him and he can help you get the body away to bury in the corner of the park."

"No, I won't put you in danger. This is all on my shoulders. I'm the one who caused it." He turned away from her. "Go back to the inn, Mercy."

She touched his shoulder, pulling. "I wish you'd give it up, but if you won't, I intend to help. He won't shoot an unarmed girl."

Jonah drew his eyebrows together and said nothing

for a bit. "All right, then, I'll slip off thataway and creep up from behind the tree. You watch and come out when I'm ready." He hunched his body for low movement, but then he reached out to touch her arm. "What will you do?"

She laughed nervously. "I'll ask him has he seen my daft brother. I'll tell him I'm worried about my brother, and I'll cry. It won't be hard, Jonah."

He began to move then, making a large, silent circle in the night. He was almost at the tree when Mercy appeared in the circle of light made by the lantern that hung on the tree.

"Sir," she called. "Have you seen a boy? My brother is lost, and I'm near about out of my mind with worry."

"How old is he, miss?"

"Near fourteen, but he's not overbig for his age." She covered her face with her hands. "He's not exactly right, in the head, I mean."

Listening, Jonah shrugged. He couldn't fault Mercy for the true words. Then the soldier did what Jonah had hoped for, stepped away from the tree, and Jonah moved, more quickly than he had ever moved before.

His hands found the musket, and with it pointed, he stepped in front of the guard. "What the —"

"It's him!" called Mercy. "I've found my senseless brother!"

The boy jabbed the musket toward the guard. "Cut him down," said the boy. "Climb up that tree, and use the knife you've got in that scabbard."

Anna Myers

The guard did not move. "You're that boy, the one who said he was your teacher."

Jonah saw then that he was the soldier with the red blotch on his face, and he remembered his kindness. "I am, and I aim to see him buried in a decent grave."

The guard pointed toward the tents. "Someone will hear or see. They ain't all asleeping."

"I'll chance it. My sister will hold the gun when he's down, and you will help me. I've a shovel over there in a good spot."

"And if I refuse? What will you do then?"

"I'll shoot you," said the boy, and he moved the musket closer.

The guard shook his head. "You ain't the kind to kill. Besides, then they'd come running for sure and certain. What good would that do your schoolmaster?" The guard folded his arms across his chest. "I won't do it."

A great weariness came over Jonah, and he feared he would stumble and drop the gun. He leaned against the tree. "What am I to do, then?" It was not a question for his listeners, but for himself. "God in heaven, what am I to do?"

The guard stepped forward and took the musket from the boy's hand. "Go home," he said. "On the morrow, he will be cut down and buried. It is the time that it must be done. I'll be on the detail along with two others, neither hard-hearted. We will be gentle, wrap him up, we will, and bury him here in the park."

"Will his grave be marked? I'd like to visit it someday."

"No," said the soldier. "There will be no mark, and soon

200

grass will cover the spot. If only grass could cover our wounds, all the wounds from this cruel war, as quick as it does the graves of them that have fallen."

"Thank you, sir," said Mercy, and taking the boy by the arm, she led him away. "Come back to the inn with me please, Jonah. You can leave at first light. There's no need to see Mister Samuel."

The boy let himself be led, but then he remembered. "There's the shovel to return," he said, and he pointed in the right direction.

They said nothing until the shovel was back in the shed. "You'll come with me now? We need to get some sleep," she said.

"I'll come. It's no matter, seeing Mister Samuel. All the hate has gone out of me, Sister, all of the hate and of all the strength too. I'm beaten."

"You'll feel better when we are in London. Oh, it will be fine to be away from all this war."

And so Jonah slept that night in a comfortable bed. Next morning, he came into the dining room and saw Mr. Samuel at breakfast. He looked tired, with heavy lines about his eyes and mouth. "I don't hate you for what you did, sir, not anymore," said Jonah, and he walked to the table.

"I'm glad." Samuel Hale brushed his hand across his face. "Would that I could forgive myself." His voice was little more than a whisper. "I did what I thought was right, Jonah, but who can say? My heart does not feel like the heart of a righteous man." He gestured toward a chair.

"You should eat. We've a long journey, and the food aboard a sailing vessel is not often pleasing."

They ate together, and when the meal was finished, Jonah asked Mr. Samuel for paper, a pen, and some ink. "I've a letter to write, sir, quite a long one." And the request was fulfilled.

Later they all rode to the pier. Inside the coach, little Tobias kept repeating, "Ride on ship, ride on ship." Jonah did not speak at all.

When time came to board, Jonah was last to leave the coach. He lifted his father's sea chest to his shoulder. He carried it across the wooden walkway, but he set it down on the deck. His sister walked in front of him, and he reached for her arm. She turned back to him. "Please keep the chest for me, Mercy. I have to say good-bye now."

"No, oh no, Jonah! You said you would come." Her hands closed around his arm.

"I said only that I would go with you to the ship. I never planned to sail to England, Mercy. I can't."

Mister Samuel and Miss Jayne had turned toward him too. "Is it because of what I did?" Mr. Samuel asked. "Does that stop you from going with us?"

"No. I meant what I said about forgiving you, but I . . ." He shook his head and looked about him, his eyes searching. "I don't know how to say it exactly." He shrugged. "I am an American, that's all. I didn't want to take a side in all this, but . . . I have no choice. I'll do what I can for America's cause."

"We can't change your mind?" Miss Jayne asked, and

when he shook his head, she leaned over to kiss his cheek.

Mister Samuel put out his hand, and Jonah shook it. "You can always go back to Stone Croft, at least as long as it belongs to me. It is your home."

"Thank you, sir. Thank you for all you have done for us."

"We'll take Tobias below to see our quarters," said Miss Jayne.

Jonah was left with his sister still holding to his arm. "Jonah, oh, Jonah, how can I leave you?" Tears rolled down her cheeks.

"You've no choice." He pulled away his arm, and then he hugged her close. "Write to me by way of Missus Green at the New London newspaper. I'll do the same wherever I go, and she can forward our letters to each other."

"And where is that? Where is it you go?" She stepped away from him, wiped at her tears, then touched his cheek.

"I'll go to General Washington. They say he's camped at Harlem Heights, six miles to the north. I'll do whatever I can. If they won't let me fight, I'll clean their tents or shine their boots or carry their water."

"I've a bit of money." She put her hand into her pocket, drew out something, and pressed it into his hand. "Take it, and be careful, Jonah."

He nodded and smiled. "I will. I'll be watchful of the whale." He did not stay to see the ship sail. Instead, he went back to the inn and secured permission to sit for a time at a table. Then he took the writing materials from his pocket and began to write. "I want the people of New

London and of all the world to know that on the 22nd day of September 1776, Captain Nathan Hale of the Continental army resigned his life, a sacrifice to his country's liberty, in New York."

For a long time, Jonah sat writing. He wrote of the soldier's bravery and of his last words. When finally the writing was done, he rose, found a place to post the letter, and began to walk north.

CHAPTER EIGHTEEN

The Beginning

Jonah walked that day, stopping only once to drink from a stream that he found bubbling over rocks. He drank, and he rested for a time. He could not linger long. Something pulled him. Just as night fell, he came to the top of a hill and saw them below him. The American army camped before him. By the light of the September moon and the light from their fires, he saw their tents, white in the night, row after row of them. He felt proud seeing those tents, but he also felt afraid.

He walked on and soon a voice called out, "Halt! Who goes there?" A soldier stepped from the shadows, and his musket pointed at Jonah.

"My name is Jonah Hawkins," he said, "and I want to join the army."

"You're but a boy. You're too small to fight. Go home to your mother." The soldier's voice was not unkind, but he waved Jonah away.

"My mother is dead, as is my father. Once I had a teacher, but I just saw him die. The British hanged him, they did, and I want to take his place." He was surprised by how strong his voice sounded in his own ears.

"Nathan Hale? Are you talking about Captain Nathan Hale?"

"I am," said Jonah.

"Then you should wait," said the soldier. "I know someone who might want to speak to you. My watch will be over shortly." He used his gun to point to a log. "You can wait for me there."

Jonah waited, and then he followed the soldier, followed him through a line of guards, down the hill, and along a path between tents. Finally, the soldier stopped. "Asher," he called. He leaned down close to the flap and called again. "Asher, wake up. A boy called Jonah Hawkins is here; claims to have been there when they hanged Captain Hale."

Asher Wright came out of the tent, rubbing sleep from his eyes. "Jonah Hawkins," he said, "I am amazed. I thought I would have to look for you after this war is over, and here you stand!" Asher went back into his tent, and when he came out he handed Jonah the copy of *Cato*. They talked then, sitting beside the fire for half the night. Jonah found it strangely easy to talk to this man. Asher told him about how he came to have the book, and Jonah told Asher how he watched Nathan Hale die.

"A Redcoat named Montresor came to tell us," Asher explained, "under a flag of truce. He said Nathan waited in his tent and that he wrote letters. Montresor doubted, though, that the letters would ever get delivered." Asher shrugged. "One of them could never be. He wrote one to Colonel Knowlton, not knowing the colonel had been killed in battle already. Montresor told it just like you did, word for word what Nathan said."

They talked more, Jonah telling about his life in New London, about how Master Hale taught, and about the barrels. Asher told about Coventry and about how he and Nathan had been boys together. Finally, Jonah had the nerve to ask the question. "Can I stay here?" He held his breath for a second, then went on. "I'd like to join the army if they will let me. I'm almost fourteen."

Asher shook his head. "It's not up to me. I'm just a nobody private, but I'll ask. I'll ask a captain." He looked up at the sky. "Not much time left till morning, but you can spend what's left of it sleeping in this tent. There's room for one more.

Early the next morning, Asher took Jonah to see a man named Captain West. "Near fourteen, huh?" The captain sat at a small table in a tent, and he looked critically at Jonah, who stood before him. "I'd say that's too young, and besides you're scrawny."

"I'm a hard worker, though, I am, and stronger than I look." Jonah bit at his lip. "If I can't fight, can I at least stay here, do things, you know, that would help the army?"

The captain sighed. "Well, might not be any harm in letting you stay about, that is, if you are really a worker. Lord knows this army has lots of hangers-on, women and children following after us." He leaned back in his chair studying Jonah. "There's something about you, boy, something that makes me think you're made sturdy. Tell you what. If you work hard and last it out till you're fifteen, I'll sign you up to be a soldier."

"Thank you, sir. I am beholden to you. I'll last it out. I need to be a soldier, need it awful bad."

It was that very evening that he saw General Washington. Jonah had been told to take firewood to add to the fire in front of the big white tent. He was moving a stick to throw in when the general lifted the flap and came out.

Jonah froze, the wood still in his hand. He could feel the man's eyes on him, and he wished he could run. Who was he to be standing in front of George Washington's tent? What was a boy supposed to do in the presence of a general? He felt inclined to bow, but he knew that it was not the American thing to do. He kept his eyes down and tried to make himself small and unobtrusive.

"Are you that boy I heard about?" Washington moved to stand near Jonah. "The one who saw Nathan Hale die?"

"I am, sir. He was my schoolmaster."

"Tell me your name, young man."

"Jonah Hawkins, sir."

"Do you remember Captain Hale's last words, Jonah?"

"I do, sir. They will sound in my ears always."

"In mine too, Jonah. Oh yes, in mine too." The general turned then and went back into his tent as Jonah added his small log to the blazing fire.

Author's Note

I absolutely loved writing about Nathan Hale. My sisters and I traveled to Connecticut, where we saw his schoolhouses in East Haddam and in New London. We also visited the family home in Coventry, where I saw Nathan's leather army trunk. I am grateful to the Connecticut people who worked hard to preserve these sites and to keep them open for visitors.

Nathan Hale really did teach girls for free in New London from five thirty until seven thirty in the morning. He really was a very accomplished athlete and was able to jump from one barrel to another. He could also kick a ball very high. I read many letters written to him and from him. I also read what people who knew him well wrote about him. Over and over he was described as a handsome young man who was well liked. His friends did try to dissuade him from volunteering as a spy for George Washington. We have no record definitely saying that Nathan Hale ever met General Washington, but it seems likely that he did. The general did visit the Shaw home in New London, but that visit occurred later and would have been too late for Nathan Hale to have met him there.

It is true that Nathan Hale had a large brown mole on his neck, and his boyhood friends did tease him by saying he would probably hang. John Montresor, aide-de-camp to General William Howe, did invite Nathan Hale into his tent and allow him to write two letters, one to his brother Enoch and one to Lieutenant Colonel Knowlton, who had been killed while Nathan Hale was behind British lines. Enoch Hale mentioned in his diary that Montresor came to the American soldiers to tell about Nathan's death. His dying words were repeated to the patriots and recorded by one of Nathan's friends.

Did Nathan Hale really say exactly, "I only regret that I have but one life to lose for my country"? No one knows for sure, but it seems likely to me that these words were at least very close to what he said. Those words were a paraphrase of lines from the play *Cato,* and Nathan Hale was a lover of literature. Also, he had the entire night before he was hanged to decide on his speech.

Jonah and Mercy Hawkins are totally fictional characters. Most researchers agree that Nathan Hale was probably reported to the British by his cousin Samuel Hale, who did work for the British in New York. No one knows for sure, but Nathan's father seems to have believed it was Samuel. I learned nothing about the real Samuel Hale except that he went to England to live shortly after

Nathan's death. My character Samuel was not based on fact.

We do not know the exact spot where Nathan Hale was buried in New York, but when I let Jonah write the words "resigned his life, a sacrifice to his country's liberty," I was using the words Nathan's father put on a stone erected for him in the Coventry cemetery.

Nathan Hale was a fine young person, and he died too soon. Not much has changed since 1776. Young people still die in war. Will we ever learn?